HEADWATERS REVENGE

Book 2: Overdrive Evans Series

Patrick J. Hughes

BearLilly Press

To all of the loved ones, family members, friends, and communities that enriched the author's life journey. He (aka I) will be eternally grateful.

CONTENTS

CHAPTER 1

Overdrive's Uneasy Feeling – Sunday;
September 20, 1964; 8:00 PM

J ames 'Overdrive' Evans was mystified by the way he
felt. The terrible burden he'd struggled under for
half a year, the fear of losing his multi-generation
family farm, had been lifted yesterday. Oostburg Bank
had approved the loan that'd saved he and his wife
Mary's farm. Given the circumstances, you'd think he'd
be ecstatic, but he wasn't and couldn't understand why.
When he looked in the mirror, he saw a 46-year-old
strong-jawed, six-three, slender, wiry-strong farmer in
his prime. But the churn inside was completely at odds
with this reassuring visage. The strange sense of unease
and foreboding troubled him.

Was there still something to fear from Rachel Wolf?
Clearly, Wolf wasn't someone to be trifled with. She'd
managed to maneuver he and Mary to the brink, literally
within days of losing everything, without breaking a
single law. Well, at least not until she attempted to knock
off Darkwater Flint. Overdrive's father, Old Bill, would've
been inconsolable had he lost his old friend. Hell, we

all would've been. Who knew attending Potawatomi tribal council, his own tribe's meeting, could be life-threatening? Attempt murder over a few snapshots and an audio tape? Even so, Overdrive couldn't help but admire the evil woman's intellect.

Still lost in thought, Overdrive was emptying his milking machine into a pail, when the persistent calling of his name snapped him out of his reverie. He looked up and there stood Mary, with a quizzical look on her face. Flustered, Overdrive said, "What?"

Mary gave him the stink eye, "What? Is that all you've got? I've been standing here calling your name at least a half dozen times. Where the hell were you? Daydreaming about Hilda again?"

Hilda was one of Overdrive's old flames from high school. Although he hadn't seen her since, Mary had a habit of bringing her up when trying to make a point. From past experience, Overdrive knew he'd better choose his next words carefully. He let his eyes linger on Mary, scanned her lean and shapely frame top to bottom, then said, "Well, Mary, aren't you a vision of beauty today. Why don't you do a little spin, while I enjoy the view. Hilda never had a chance, and you know it."

Mary giggled, and said, "Not bad for a socially-awkward aging farm boy."

Overdrive nodded and flickered a smile, "Sometimes I amaze even myself."

Mary rolled her eyes, "Yeah, I'm sure you do. Anyway, now that I've got your attention, I have a question."

Overdrive straightened up and found her eyes, "Okay, I'm listening."

After a head turn to verify none of the kids were

close, Mary leaned in and lowered her voice, "Do you think we should tell the kids what's been going on?"

Overdrive thought for a moment, then said softly, "When I was growing up, I was under the illusion that this farm had always been in the family, and always would be. Almost as a given, you know? I didn't realize how tenuous it all was, until you and I took over. The kids may still see it that way, and find it comforting like I did. Do we really want to ruin that for them?"

Mary's eyes widened, then she said, "Now that you put it that way, maybe not." She rose on her tiptoes, gave him a peck on the cheek, and whispered, "Pretty deep thinking, coming from a man who reeks of cow shit."

Overdrive mimed sniffing himself, and said, "Really, I can't smell a thing."

Mary winked, "Trust me, you stink." Then, unexpectedly, she added, "It felt kind of nice to give Darkwater that check today, didn't it? Without it, he'd still be dead in the water until his insurance money came through."

Matter-of-fact now, Overdrive said, "Well, speaking as a man who still trembles when breaking a $10 bill, yes and no."

Mary's eyebrows went up, "Oh my god! Seriously? Please tell me you weren't actually thinking about welshing out on Darkwater. He almost got killed because of us!"

Overdrive tap-danced, "Oh no, of course not. But you know how I am with money. It isn't easy to part with, even when I know it's coming back."

Mary's eyes twinkled, "Yes, you have earned a certain reputation over the years, haven't you? A true Welshman, through and through."

The evening milking and clean up was soon finished, and Overdrive and Mary stepped out of the milk house together, into the crisp and breezy evening. Falling leaves were visible under the sodium-vapor yard-light, and David was running circles in the backyard trying to catch them. They noticed a commotion down by the house. Peering into the dim light, they could see Marie and John, near where the sidewalk bridges a gentle swale. Marie was struggling for air, bent over in laughter. Flashlight in hand, John looked on from his hands and knees.

As Overdrive and Mary approached, Mary asked, "What's so funny?"

Marie, teary-eyed, did her best to straighten up and respond, "The ddww ..." But another spasm cut her short. After it passed, Marie held her aching sides, and tried again, "The dweeebbb ..." Involuntarily knotting up once more, all Marie could do was let it roll. Finally, after a long moment, she straightened back up, used the palms of her hands to clear her eyes, breathed deeply, and croaked, "The dweeb thinks he can train worms. He ... he's a ..." Struggling for control, Marie managed to utter, "He's a moron!"

Then, Marie lost it once more, and Overdrive and Mary turned to John, who said matter-of-factly, "For the record, they're night crawlers not worms. And whether they're trainable is an experimental question. I'm catching and releasing them now, to see if that'll make them easier to catch next spring, when I need bait to go fishing."

Overdrive's hearty laugh earned him a sharp elbow from Mary. She then bent at the waist to offer John an encouraging smile, and said in a soft voice, "I don't think that's how it works, John. Do you?"

John put on a thoughtful expression, and said, "I don't know. Like I said, it's an experimental question."

About then Kathy stuck her head out the farmhouse's back door, and said, "Popcorn's done and McHale's Navy starts in 10 minutes."

Feeling rescued, Mary shot her eldest daughter a smile, "Thank you Kathy, perfect timing." Then she pushed her big lug of a husband toward the door, and barked, "David, get in the house before you step in a hole and sprain an ankle. John, you too, the experiment will have to wait for another day. Marie, inside, and since when does a young lady in high school resort to name calling? Keep that up and you'll lose your privileges to get off the school bus in Cascade."

Marie's eyebrows shot up in alarm, "But I need grandpa's help with my freshman family history project!"

Mary said sternly, "Then watch your tongue."

Overdrive and Mary held back as the kids settled into the living room, each with their own bowl, in front of the TV. Jumbo plucked Joe off a contended chair in a headlock, and knuckled the top of his head until he agreed to give up the prime seat. After running his smart mouth for a while to save face, Joe pushed his way onto the couch. The girls made room for him, by bumping John to the floor. John relocated David to claim the prime spot on the floor. When the kids were all settled, Mary whispered to Overdrive, "You're right, James. It's best not to tell them what's been going on. Let them enjoy their childhood a little longer."

✳ ✳ ✳

Two days later, Overdrive and Mary got a call from the office of their attorney, Ted Ritter. They're told that Ted's still up north in Forest County, but he'd call them that evening, after milking's done. Overdrive spent the day chopping field corn and filling silo with his father, while Mary picked squash, and the kids were in school. Anticipation of the coming call grew as the day wore on.

The family had just come in from the barn, and was cleaning up, when the phone rang. Mary answered on the first ring, and Overdrive quickly herded the kids into the living room and shut the door. Upbeat and talking fast, Ted said, "I'm sorry for calling early, but there's a lot to cover and I didn't want to run too late."

Overdrive said, "No problem, Ted, we just got in. What've you got?"

Ted, voice animated, "First thing the morning after the bank loan celebration, Darkwater called his insurance company from my office, and introduced me as his attorney. They immediately assigned an investigator to the claim by the name of Don Schneider, and got him on the line. Real nice guy, we hit it off right away."

Mary, relief apparent in her voice, "That's sounds wonderful, Ted. Does that mean we've been wasting our worry?"

Ted chuckled, "Well, not exactly. We'll have to clear Darkwater for the arson, before they'll pay for his loss. Right now, he's the lead suspect. But Schneider was elated to hear I had a PI on the ground in Forest County, and agreed to hop in his car and meet us up there right away. I immediately called the PI, filled him in, and told him to find out who set the fire. Then I packed, and drove north."

Overdrive grunted, "Huh, that sounds encouraging."

Ted, still upbeat, "It is. Schneider and I met for dinner in Crandon last night. I told him the whole sordid tale. Rachel Wolf's Development Partners and Headwaters of the Milwaukee River shell corporations; her use of DP to partner with the Potawatomi; her need to possess your farm through DP's subsidiary, HMR; the plan for the casino, and so on. Before dessert arrived, Schneider had become an ally. He understood that we'd already done a lot of his work for him."

Mary praised, "That's incredible, Ted, well done."

Ted, on a roll, "It gets better. Schneider offered to take me along to his meeting this morning with the fire marshal. We met at the scene of the fire, and to avoid questions, he introduced me as his trainee. The guy explained to us what happened, and showed us the proof that caused him to reach that conclusion. A window at the back of the house had been broken, and accelerant and a flame tossed in. The same had happened to the car's passenger-side front window."

Overdrive muttered, "So, if Darkwater had been home, he'd be a dead man."

Ted admitted, "It looks that way, James. The fire marshal said the house was old dry wood and basically went poof." After a pause to let that sink in, Ted continued, "I arranged for my PI to join Schneider and me for lunch. Schneider heard firsthand about the manhunt for Darkwater, and was so impressed with the PI's story, he offered to seek internal approval for covering the PI's costs. About an hour ago, I learned the insurance company had agreed."

After a moment of empty air, Overdrive blurted, "Wait a minute. You mean we won't be billed at all for the PI? I mean, the PI started after the fire, right? When

Darkwater missed his rendezvous with the courier."

Mary scoffed, "Oh, for crumb sakes, James. Let's hear Ted out, and worry about the penny-pinching later."

Ted verified the entire PI tab was covered, then continued, "This afternoon, I tagged along with Schneider to his meeting in Crandon with the Forest County Sherriff. According to him, early on the second day after the fire, tribal police requested their assistance in a manhunt for an arsonist on the run. Such requests weren't unusual, his office and the tribal police backed each other up regularly. The county's role was to setup road blocks around Crandon. But early the next day, the local quarry called in a breaking and entering. A private road had been breached that bypassed one of the roadblocks, and the arsonist slipped away. When the Sherriff passed that along to the tribe, they told him to stand down. Later that day the tribe discovered the arsonist had rented a car in Crandon, which meant they had the make and model of the getaway car. The Sherriff expected to hear a statewide bolo come over the wire, but it never did. This surprised him, but not his problem."

After a moment to process, Mary said, "You'd think the Sherriff would've thought it odd to be chasing the owner of the torched property. I mean, an owner wouldn't set a fire for insurance money, and then run. How stupid would that be?"

Ted conceded, "That's a great point, Mary. The same thought occurred to Schneider during the meeting, and he asked the Sherriff point blank. The guy had no idea they'd been chasing the owner. Anyway, after that Schneider and I met with the chief of tribal police. According to him, very early on the morning after the fire, he'd been directed by the chairman of tribal council, to work with DP to find Darkwater. Apparently, the fire had been declared arson, Darkwater was the prime suspect, and he needed to be apprehended. The chairman told him DP had volunteered to assist, because they and the tribe were now partners. The casino needed state approvals, and those might be jeopardized if the state heard rumors that the tribe was unable to maintain law and order."

Mary blew a stray hank of hair from her face, "It sounds like the tribe is nothing more than Wolf's puppet already."

Like-minded, Ted said, "Exactly. She fed them a line of bullshit and they ate it right up. Anyway, the chief confirmed they picked up Darkwater's trail at Robin's house, lost him, brought in dogs, picked up the trail again, tracked him into the national forest, and whatnot. Everything he said about how Darkwater slipped away was consistent with the Sherriff's story. At the end, Schneider played dumb, and asked why they hadn't put out a statewide bolo. After an awkward hesitation, the chief claimed he had no information on the vehicle, and couldn't."

Overdrive interrupted, "That's not what the Sherriff said."

Ted chuckled, "Exactly, he was caught off guard, and lied. Anyway, tonight Schneider and I had dinner with the PI again. Guess what? Behind Darkwater's house, there's a large wooded area, and then another road. According to eye witnesses, two powerful-looking black cars were seen parked on that road the night of the fire. The descriptions resembled what he'd seen the DP guys driving, so the PI did a little research, and ran down a photo of a Dodge 880 Police Pursuit Vehicle. The witnesses all provided positive ID, when shown the photo. That baby has a 413 cubic-inch 4-barrel V-8 engine, and hits 125 mph on the straightaway."

Overdrive whistled, "Holy shit!"

Excited now, Ted continued, "Exactly! And it gets better. The PI found a deer trail that led from that road, through the woods, to the back of Darkwater's property. Along the trail, there's an enormous tree, and in it a large permanent deer-stand. The stand appeared regularly used, so he staked it out. Shortly after school let out, a teenage couple came along and climbed up and in. From the sounds of it they were fooling around, so the PI climbed up and rudely interrupted. Caught in the act, the kids became extremely cooperative. They'd been up the tree the night of the fire, heard noises, and in the dim-moonlight saw four big men walking in the direction of Darkwater's house, arms straight and swaying as if carrying heavy burdens. A few minutes later, they heard a big whap, and saw an orange glow from that direction. Soon after the men returned, moving fast and holding high and out of the way, empty five-gallon cans."

Mary gasped in disbelief, "Oh my god, you've got proof already?"

Ted, in a confidant tone, "It looks that way, Mary. Schneider thinks this might be all he needs, but just to be sure, we're meeting with the chairman of tribal council in the morning. Meanwhile, the PI will seek more corroborating witnesses. I plan to head back to Random Lake tomorrow afternoon. We should talk again tomorrow evening. I'll call you again, after milking."

* * *

When Ted called the following evening, Overdrive and Mary had just finished shooing the kids into the living room with a plate of apple nut bars. In the kitchen, they each picked up their receivers on the first ring and chorused, "Hello."

Ted, even more hyped than the night before, "Overdrive, Mary ... greetings. There's a lot to cover, so let me dive in. The chairman of tribal council, a fellow named Long Body, knew we'd already met with his police chief, and promised both his and the chief's full cooperation. In his view, when Darkwater ran it proved his guilt. He said he's motivated to help Schneider wrap up his investigation quickly, because the success of a new tribal initiative depends on it. As he put it, the initiative required state approvals, and only a quick resolution would guarantee them. When asked about the state-wide bolo, he repeated the same lie."

Overdrive harrumphed, "That figures."

Ted pressed on, "Schneider also asked why DP had participated in the manhunt. Smooth as silk, Long Body said DP had skin in the game as a partner on the pending initiative, and by chance had resources in the area."

Mary asked, "Is that even legal? Vigilante's, I mean."

Ted chuckled, "Not in Wisconsin. But on federal tribal lands, who knows. Anyway, you'll love this. When we appeared unsatisfied with that answer, Long Body expressed his certainty that the owner of DP, Rachel Wolf, would also be happy to cooperate fully with the investigation."

Overdrive exploded, "Are you shitting me? He actually said that?"

Ted, in an excited tone, "Schneider's got it on tape! He's got all these meetings on tape. We finally have someone on record saying Rachel Wolf owns DP. Even better, by offering up Wolf's name to us, Long Body essentially admitted the tribe has no idea she set the fire. If true, that means we can seek justice for Darkwater against Wolf, and Wolf alone."

Relieved, Mary gushed, "Oh thank god! I'd been worrying over whether the tribe would take Darkwater back. Maybe holding them harmless will help."

Ted, somewhat more cautious, "Well, let's not get ahead of ourselves. Freeing the tribe from fire loss liability will help, but there's still the matter of no casino revenue any time soon. Anyway, after the meeting, Schneider and I met with the PI again, before I drove south. He found four more witnesses, although only one may be reliable. Apparently, four tribesmen in their late-20s drove past the two parked cars on the night of the fire, on their way home from celebrating. The driver has a health issue and doesn't drink, but the other three were wasted. According to the driver, when his headlights first hit the cars, both trunks were open and four men were milling about. Instantly, the trunks slammed shut, and the men appeared uncertain what to do, so they just stood there and waved awkwardly as the car passed. The driver claimed he'd seen those men at tribal council."

Overdrive muttered, "Hell, that should be plenty for Schneider."

Ted, with caution in his voice, "Schneider believes it is. But just to be clear, we still have a touchy situation here, that'll require more thought and some tough decisions. It'd be best to get everybody together in person. Darkwater says he can come south this weekend. Peter Nyenhuis from Oostburg Bank has agreed to make himself available. I'm hoping you two and Old Bill can come as well. I know this is an odd mix of people, but it's a long story best explained at the meeting. I'm thinking Saturday afternoon might work best, can you make it?"

Overdrive, now grim, "If you say it's important, we'll be there."

CHAPTER 2

Team Overdrive Makes a Choice –
Wednesday; September 23, 1964; 10:30
PM

T ed's invite list for the Saturday meeting had Overdrive and Mary feeling unsettled. Why was the bank president coming? Was their loan no longer a done deal? After a night of fitful sleep, on Thursday it took all the discipline they could muster to stay focused on their harvest tasks. Friday morning, Old Bill told them Darkwater had called, and he'd be arriving in Cascade that evening about 7:00 PM. Plans were set for the four of them to meet after milking at Harbor Lights, the rustic resort on nearby Lake Ellen.

When Overdrive and Mary walked into Harbor Lights, Old Bill and Darkwater were just finishing dinner. Old Bill waved them over for a heartfelt greeting, and after the niceties, Overdrive went to the bar and fetched a round of beers. Darkwater helped Mary pull up two more chairs, and once everyone was settled, Overdrive asked, "Darkwater, how's your new life?"

Darkwater mimed a shudder, and said, "Yeah, about

that. It's been way more cloak and dagger than I expected. Ted advised extreme caution, and I've taken him seriously. Now I'm paranoid about everything."

Mary's eyebrows went up, "Really? What do you mean?"

Darkwater leaned in, "Well, take where to live, for example. Oh, by the way, Robin and I had that talk ..." he paused to wink, "... and she moved in with me."

Mary smiled and winked back, "Good for you, Darkwater!"

Darkwater nodded, "Thanks, I appreciate that. Anyway, I originally planned to just rent a cabin at the resort. But it's common knowledge among the tribe that my guide business is run out of there, so Ted nixed that idea. Instead, we've rented a cabin in a secluded area nearby."

Overdrive, eyebrows up, "Huh, so Ted's still concerned about your safety?"

Darkwater bobbed his head, "Oh, yeah. In fact, he pumped me for details about my business. He wanted to see my advertising materials, customer lists, and whatnot. It felt like I was being interrogated."

Old Bill's eyebrows shot up, "Really? What's that all about?"

Darkwater sighed, "Ted believes Wolf's minions may still be after me. An obvious ploy would be to pose as a client. But after seeing my brochure, Ted relaxed a little. The business is billed as Trophy Guides, the images are all fish and game, and the contact information is for the resort, not me personally. The brochure even refers to me as Trophy Hound, rather than by my real name. Even repeat customers only know me as Trophy Hound."

Old Bill chuckled, "Trophy Hound, that's a good

one."

Brow wrinkled, Mary said thoughtfully, "Well, that all sounds safe enough."

Darkwater sipped his beer, and nodded, "Yep, Ted saw no need to change any of that. But he's pretty persuasive, and he did talk me into a new client meet-up protocol, and helped arm-twist the resort owner, Barney Swanson, to go along with it. Before all this crazy shit happened, whether the client was to hunt or fish, I'd always simply meet them at the resort and provide transport by boat to wherever. There's plenty of places to take them. The Eagle River area has 28 connected lakes and probably 100 islands, all accessible by boat. Most of the islands and much of the shoreline is public, and it's all surrounded by big chunks of public land. With the new protocol, Barney and I pick a different remote island for each client, and he ferries them there and picks them up afterward. From there, I use my boat to zip them around. If it's multi-day, the island becomes base camp."

Overdrive shook his head, "That sounds like a giant pain in the ass for Swanson. What's in it for him?"

Darkwater chuckled, "Trophy Guides brings in most of the resort's repeat business. Plus, it's really not a big deal for him. He's got a bunch of kids old enough to run the boats, and if school is in session, the drop-offs and pick-ups are generally before and after school anyway. If not, he or his wife do it."

Overdrive tapped Mary's forearm, "See honey, we're not the only parents preparing their children for the real world by teaching them how to work."

Mary gave him the stink eye, "Oh shush up, James. I can listen to your bullshit anytime. Let's hear what Darkwater has to say."

The three men laughed, then Darkwater continued, "Anyways, let's see, what else? Oh yeah, at Ted's urging we set up a post office box for our mail, and got an unlisted phone number. Remind me to give those to you. He also told me to brief my band's elder, Make Wit, on what'd happened and why Robin and I were hiding. When I did, the response I got was interesting. Make Wit credited me with protecting the band's sacred lands, and said he owed me a debt of gratitude. He gave his word that the band would protect us, if ever protection was needed. He also promised to spread the word among the band to stay tightlipped if anybody came around asking about us. Make Wit's word is as good as gold."

Old Bill whistled, "Wow, Ted's left no stone unturned."

Darkwater held up a finger, "Oh, I almost forgot. Boy, you're all going to love this. One day Ted asked me to drive him around to isolated picnic areas near Eagle River. He wanted to see ones that weren't well known to the general public. When we found what he was looking for, he explained. He said this picnic area is perfect because it's reachable from two directions, and easy to see approaching vehicles from either way. He wants Robin and I to limit our social interactions to daylight meet-ups with friends and relatives here, and here only. He told me to always know what vehicle our visitors would be driving. If they're tailed or a different vehicle comes, we're to jump in my car and run. Ted was dead serious. He even made me promise to explore both exit directions, and preplan at least three ways to disappear along each escape route before a faster car could overtake me. We also had to promise to keep where we lived a secret, until he said otherwise."

Old Bill lowered his voice and muttered, "Sonofabitch!"

* * *

Troubled by what Darkwater had revealed, Overdrive slept poorly and yawned his way through Saturday's morning milking. But coffee and breakfast perked him up, and afterword he walked Jumbo and Joe out to the silos, and talked them through what needed to be done to keep the silo filling moving along.

Once Jumbo and Joe were rolling, Overdrive returned to the house for his two younger sons. Unapologetic for rudely interrupting Saturday morning cartoons, Overdrive proceeded to march John and David out to the barn. There, he told them to clean the shit out of the four box stalls, and re-bed them with fresh straw. Never happy at the possibility of boys being idle, he also suggested they clean all the drinking cups from one end of the barn to the other, before dinner. When the boys eyed him in disbelief, Overdrive let his stare linger until they realized this hadn't been merely a suggestion. Afterward, Overdrive spent the rest of the morning making the rounds to the old Lemke, Adcock, and Ulbricht farms, to check on the health of his young cattle.

While Overdrive was busy spinning up the boys, Mary was doing the same with the girls. After the mountain of shit-covered laundry was washed, Kathy and Marie were to hang the clothes outside on the line to dry, and then clean the house from top to bottom. Satisfied that her girls were productively occupied, Mary headed to the orchard to inspect her apples. She judged the Jonathon apples would be ready to pick the following week, and the Idared apples about two weeks after that. Mary spent the rest of the morning in the garden, picking squash and digging a sample of potatoes to see how they're progressing.

After lunch, Overdrive and Mary headed to Ted's law office in Random Lake. Old Bill and Darkwater pulled into the parking lot just ahead of them, and Peter's car was already there. When they all walked in, Ted's assistant showed them to the conference room, where Ted and Peter waited.

After exchanging pleasantries, Ted said, "Thank you all for coming. With the exception of Old Bill, everybody's already up to speed on what I learned up north. So, I'd …"

Darkwater interrupted, "Ted, I spent last night at Old Bill's, and took the liberty of telling him everything I knew."

Ted winked, "Excellent, that'll save some time. Okay, so let's review the basic facts. Darkwater's insurance company assigned his claim to an investigator named Schneider, who's concluded that DP set the fire. Schneider has the Potawatomi tribal council chairman, a fellow named Long Body, on tape saying Rachel Wolf owns DP. In other words, the fire was set at Wolf's direction. In a perfect world, she'd be found guilty of attempted murder in a court of law, and held liable for Darkwater's loss."

Encouraged, Darkwater said, "So, you think the tribe can be left out of it?"

Ted bobbed his head, "I do. Also on tape is Long Body's assertion that Wolf would be happy to cooperate with Schneider's investigation. I doubt he'd have said that, if he knew Wolf set the fire."

Darkwater rolled his figure, "But like you say, it's not

a perfect world."

Ted, now grim, "No, it isn't. Schneider knows Darkwater is innocent, and if it were up to him, the claim would be paid immediately. But in arson cases, his company tends to drag their feet, while working to force someone to make them whole. In this case, the make-whole target is Wolf, and criminal charges, a civil suit, or a settlement are all options. From the insurance company's point of view, cornering Wolf into a settlement is quickest and has the least risk. If criminal charges are pursued, it's certainly within Wolf's means to create a circle of corruption large enough to escape them. Modest sums go a long way in hardscrabble places like Forest County. On the other hand, presuming a fair trial could be found, we'd have Wolf dead to rights. Putting her behind bars is the only sure way to get her off our backs, once and for all. With or without a criminal trial, I also believe we could make Darkwater a rich man by winning a civil suit."

After a moment of empty air, Peter said, "Ted, you've obviously been thinking about this a lot longer than we have. What do you recommend?"

Ted exhaled heavily, and said, "The Wolf family has been preying on honest, hardworking people around here since territorial days, long before statehood. They've never been brought to justice. No doubt, pursuing criminal charges is the moral and ethical thing to do. In a fair trial, we'd have enough evidence to convict."

When Ted paused, Peter prompted, "But ..."

Ted, solemnly, "But I can't in good conscience recommend criminal charges unless everybody in this room agrees. That's why you're all here."

Confused, Overdrive asked, "Why's that, Ted? You're the lawyer."

Ted leaned in, "Two reasons. First, as a practical matter, the road to victory by trial, criminal or civil, is longer than I can afford to wait for a payday. My practice isn't big enough to cover the float on something like that. James, what I'll get from the proceeds of your loan with Peter only catches me up for past work."

Overdrive nodded, "Okay, I get that."

Peter stared hard at Ted, "What's the other reason?"

Ted sighed, "Danger to Darkwater."

Mary snapped, "What?"

Ted took a deep breath, and explained, "Think about it from Wolf's point of view. Right now, Darkwater's a loose end. But she isn't motivated to do anything about it, because as far as she knows, the Evans farm becomes hers on September 30th and she'll be free to pursue the casino. As we all know, that won't happen. And when it doesn't, she'll be furious. There's a good chance she'll go after Darkwater then and there. To head that off, we've got to give her a better path forward by the end of the month. The better path, would be for her to agree to a settlement. Among the terms would be Darkwater's safety, and her making the insurance company whole. Criminal charges and a civil suit would serve as the 'or else' if she snubbed the settlement, or later violated its terms."

Old Bill frowned, and said, "So, you're recommending we settle?"

Ted shook his head, "Well, not exactly. I'm merely pointing out that for Darkwater, the safest and quickest way back to his old life is to settle. Morally and ethically? We should press criminal charges, and put Wolf behind bars. If we go that route, we might as well bring a civil suit too, and make Darkwater a rich man."

Darkwater smiled and rubbed his chin, "I kind of

like the sound of being rich. How much less safe would I be, if we tried for that?"

Ted, grimmer than before, "If we do anything but settle, you'd probably have to spend the rest of your life in witness protection. Starting like … now."

Darkwater recoiled, "You're shitting me, right?"

Startled by a negative thought, Old Bill demanded, "What guarantees my friend's safety, even if we settle?"

Ted's eyes narrowed, "As part of the settlement, we'll all have to sign NDAs preventing us from disclosing our evidence about the fire and its underlying motivation, the Evans farm swindle. But if Wolf violated any term of the settlement, we'd be released from those NDAs. Like I said before, our biggest hammer is the threat of criminal charges and a civil suit, over the fire. But don't forget the noise we'd be able to make, over her attempt to steal a dairy farm to build a casino. After a news cycle like that, any future casino proposal by her would be DOA at the state, and the bruhaha might even jeopardize her regional bank. We'll also make it clear that Darkwater isn't the only key witness that can bury her in court. At this point, dozens of people … everybody in this room, the entire Oostburg Bank board, the PI, Schneider and others at the insurance company … all have the goods on her. There's safety in numbers. She can't kill all of us."

Mary, agitated, "I hope you're sure about that."

Ted paused a moment, then said with confidence, "I'm as sure as I can be. Wolf didn't get to where she is today, by being crazy."

Peter pointed a finger at him, "You know what? You ARE a sly bastard!"

Impenitent, Ted joked, "I'll take that as a compliment." The discussion continued, around and around, without resolution. At Ted's suggestion, they decided to sleep on it, and reconvene the following afternoon.

Out in the parking lot, Overdrive, Mary, Old Bill and Darkwater huddled up and eyed each other, all with the same thought on their mind. Mary was the first to say it out loud, "We need to consult with the Welsh ancestors."

Old Bill has an unusual gift, the ability to use a simple ritual to open and close a communication bridge with his deceased Welsh ancestors. When open, he speaks freely with them in Welsh, and can access anything they've learned during their lifetimes. Skeptical at first, Overdrive became a true believer when the ancestors helped save the farm from Rachel Wolf. Currently, he and Old Bill were the only living souls that knew the ritual. However, Mary and Darkwater also believe, and have participated in bridges as living-side monitors in the past.

Plans were set to bridge to the ancestors that evening, after milking. On the way to the car, Overdrive pulled his father off to the side, found his eyes, and said in a low voice, "Dad, I've been giving it some thought, and I think it's time to include Mary and Darkwater in the ritual. If anything happened to you, we'd lose our ability to bridge. I'm not the type to become fluent in Welsh, but somebody's got to. Maybe one of them could do it. As living-side monitors, they only hear us, and miss out on the ancestor's voices. Having the full experience might motivate one of them to put in the effort."

Old Bill looked at his son, reevaluating. Then he nodded, "When we get back to the shack, I'll send Darkwater on an errand, dial up the ancestors, and ask."

* * *

Old Bill saw the headlights when Overdrive and Mary pulled up to the shack that evening, and from the door, yelled for both to come in. After they entered, he asked them to take a seat and locked the door behind them. In the small living area were two stuffed chairs, with a small table between. Facing them, were two kitchen chairs, also with a small table between. On each table were two cocktail glasses and a bottle. Darkwater was seated in one of the stuffed chairs and the other was Old Bill's, so Overdrive and Mary sat opposite.

Overdrive noticed the surprise on Mary's face, when she realized the ritual would occur with her in the room. He smiled as she looked around, took note of the drawn window shades, and scanned the darkened shack filled with dancing shadows caused by the dim candle light.

With a serious expression, Old Bill leaned forward and caught first Darkwater's and then Mary's eye, "The ancestors have granted their permission for you two to be here. I'll walk you through what you need to do to participate, and then we'll bridge."

Eyes wide, Mary and Darkwater nodded their understanding.

Old Bill picked up the bottle on the table nearest him, and said in an instructional tone, "This is *Drysien Gwyllt*, a Welsh liquor. It's made with what they call wild brambles, or blackberries, that're fermented and marinated in spirits. To open the bridge, all of us must alternately sip this, and whisper the Welsh phrase '*a fo ben, bid bont*', which means *if you want to be a leader, be a bridge*." Old Bill set down the bottle, and leaned in even further, "It's important to properly pronounce the Welsh phrase. We'll have to practice it, until you get it right."

Old Bill had Mary and Darkwater whisper '*a fo ben, bid bont*' over and over, correcting them as they went, until he judged the enunciation to be adequate. Then Old Bill picked up his bottle, poured jiggers of the dark liquid into the glasses for he and Darkwater, and motioned for Overdrive to do the same. Once everyone was glass-to-lips, all four began sipping *Drysien Gwyllt* and whispering '*a fo ben, bid bont*', over and over, and within a minute the bridge to the Welsh ancestors was opened.

As Old Bill began speaking in Welsh, Overdrive studied Mary and Darkwater intently, and enjoyed their eye-bulge reaction when the ancestors talked back. Having experienced it himself, he knew exactly how they felt. The eerie sense of a new presence, the candles suddenly more brilliant, the voices speaking gibberish … er … Welsh. Not Old Bill's voice, but other voices.

Old Bill shared with the ancestors what'd been learned in Ted's office that afternoon, and why they felt conflicted about what to do. He emphasized that a decision was needed by tomorrow, and asked for their advice. As Old Bill laid it out, the intensity of the ancestral chatter ebbed and flowed. When he finished, their chatter continued on its own, and then he started fielding their questions.

Before long, Old Bill sat back, "They've asked a question I don't have a good answer for. All the evidence seems to tie the fire to DP. Why's Ted so sure he'd be able to hold Wolf accountable for anything they might do?"

The three silent living eyed each other, then Overdrive volunteered, "Well, Long Body's on tape saying the owner of DP is Rachel Wolf."

After passing that along, Old Bill paused for the chatter, and when it died down turned to Overdrive, "They're not convinced. They think any Wolf that lived up to the family name, would simply finger a fall guy at DP, and pay him handsomely for his trouble."

Darkwater conceded, "Huh, good point. But Ted seemed pretty certain he'd be able to convict Wolf. Maybe he's got something else."

Mary winced and said, "You can't risk your life on a maybe."

Overdrive raised his hand, "Wait a minute, now. Ted's as good as they get. If he thinks he can get a conviction, he probably can."

Old Bill relayed these sentiments, as well as his own. After the rumble died down, he muttered to himself, "Of course, how'd I forget?" Then he looked first to Overdrive and Mary, and then to Darkwater, "There's been a saying in the Evans family for generations. *The path of life encounters many crossroads. To find your way, remember why you've been placed on earth … your mission, and choose the most direct path to it.*"

Mary, impressed, "That's pretty deep, coming from a long line of farmers."

Old Bill made a rolling motion with his index finger, "Darkwater, why're you here on earth?"

Startled, Darkwater thought for a moment, then said, "To lead clients to trophy fish and game."

Old Bill, finger still rolling, "What's your most direct path to that?"

Darkwater, palm to forehead, "A settlement."

Old Bill turned to Overdrive and Mary, "Why're you two here on earth?"

Mary, hand up to go first, "To keep the farm in the

family."

Overdrive, "And make it possible for the next generation to do the same."

Old Bill, still rolling, "What's your most direct path to that?"

Overdrive and Mary, in unison, "A settlement."

Old Bill mimed taking a bow, "You have your answer."

* * *

When everyone arrived Sunday afternoon, Ted had fresh croissants and coffee waiting in his conference room. After the niceties, Ted said, "I'd like to just go around the room, and see where everybody came down. Darkwater, you've got the most to lose, why don't you go first?"

Darkwater thought for a moment, "I want my old life back, without fear of reprisal. Having lost everything, I also need that insurance payout. If I understand correctly, a settlement is the fastest way to get there."

Face neutral, Ted motioned toward Overdrive and Mary, "What say you?"

Mary nodded to Overdrive, who said solemnly, "Thanks to the loan coming from Peter's bank, Mary and I have a farm to run. We'd like to stay focused on that. Wolf made a run at us once, but thanks to everyone in this room she failed. We'd prefer not to provoke another, and think a settlement is the best bet."

Ted looked Peter's way, and asked, "Peter, what do you think?"

Peter took a deep breath, and said, "I've polled all the board members, and believe I can speak for the bank on this one. Frankly, there'd been more support than I expected for trying to put Wolf behind bars. We hate her with a passion, and have great confidence in your legal prowess. But we knew where Darkwater and the Evans's would stand, or at least where they should stand, given their circumstances. Without them as plaintiffs, there's really no case. But even if they'd been plaintiffs, we felt you'd probably need to rely heavily on the bank for financial support. That's not something the board was prepared to take on. Our balance sheet was damaged fighting off Wolf's hostile takeover attempt, and we need to stick to our knitting for a while to recover. A settlement seems best."

Ted looked disappointed but nodded his understanding. Then, he motioned to Old Bill, "How about you?"

Old Bill leaned back in his chair, "Well, I don't really have a dog in this fight. But it's crossed my mind that it might take more than a cracker-jack country lawyer, a small independent bank, one dairy farm family, and a sportsmen's guide to bring down Rachel Wolf. No offense intended."

Ted settled back in his chair, "No offense taken. And just for the record, the insurance company wants to settle, too. Look everyone, I expected this outcome. I can't say I'm happy about it, I'd be a liar if I did. To my knowledge, there's never been a better opportunity to put a Wolf behind bars. But I understand your positions, and in your shoes would probably come to the same decision. Schneider and I've already begun drafting the settlement package. We'll write it in a way where any fool would know enough to sign. Wolf is no fool, she'll sign."

Still anxious, Darkwater asked, "After she signs, can

all the cloak and dagger go away? It's beginning to creep Robin and me out."

Ted leaned back in, and his eyes narrowed, "That's an excellent question, Darkwater. But just to be safe, I think we'd better keep it up for a while longer, until we're absolutely certain Wolf is playing ball. Schneider and I are planning a one-two punch, so she'll know we mean business. I've purposely delayed the HMR payoff until September 29th, the day before they think the farm becomes theirs. This buys the insurance company enough time to finish the settlement package, and have it delivered to Wolf the same day. We're giving her five business days to settle, before we go to the authorities and news media. As a courtesy, we'll express our willingness to meet at her earliest convenience if negotiation is necessary, but we doubt that it will be. The twin jolts of being forced to pay for the fire and losing the Evans farm, should get her to back off and leave Darkwater and the rest of us alone. Any misstep on her part risks her bank, and the opportunity to develop a casino elsewhere."

CHAPTER 3

Overdrive's Catharsis – Tuesday;
September 29, 1964; 3:00 PM

I t's mid-afternoon and Overdrive was lost in thought, while chopping field corn on a windy strip of land behind his barn at the homeplace. On the heels of last night's cold front, came the season's first high-wind arctic blast. That morning mere minutes after starting to chop, he'd retreated back to the house, shivering uncontrollably, in search of his winter gear. But once chilled, comfort generally remained elusive for the rest of the day, even when wearing a fur-lined leather trapper hat, insulated coveralls, and mitts. Today was no exception. More seasonal weather was predicted to return in a few days, and he thanked the lord for that.

Earlier, while Overdrive was in the house to warm up and have lunch, Ted called with the good news. That morning as planned, his courier delivered the Oostburg Bank cashier's check to the offices of HMR, and then brought the signed receipt back to Ted. With receipt in hand, Ted had been animated. He bragged the bastards must've shit their pants when they opened the envelope.

Even better, Ted had also received an update from Schneider. That morning, Rachel Wolf had personally received, and signed for, the insurance company's courier-delivered settlement package. The final language gave her five business days to negotiate and pay a private settlement covering Darkwater's fire insurance claims and other related costs. As justification, the cover letter referenced the results of the insurer's investigation, which had been graciously summarized and appended. The letter also asserted Wolf's motive for setting the fire, and backed that assertion by appending a summary of her efforts to force the Evans family off their farm, in order to develop a Potawatomi casino.

As outlined in the letter, should Wolf miss the deadline, the insurance company would go to the authorities and news outlets, and the truth would come out. The letter set forth the likely outcome should that happen ... Wolf facing multiple felony criminal charges, including attempted murder and bank fraud ... jail time and loss of her regional bank ... unlikely state approvals for a casino elsewhere, and so on. Alternatively, Wolf could settle on time and all parties aware of this damaging information would sign NDAs and keep it to themselves.

Giddy by the end of the call, Ted described how he and Schneider synched their deliveries so Wolf's would arrive first, followed by HMR's a half hour later. He joked that when HMR called Wolf, it'd be like tossing a lit match into a pail of gasoline. Ted, Overdrive, and Mary shared a big laugh at the thought of it, a glorious release, which they all needed. But the real release came after the call ended. Overdrive and Mary sobbed uncontrollably in each other's arms. When the dam broke, all their pent-up anxiety and resentment came spewing out.

The emotional response caught Overdrive and Mary by surprise. They'd known for nine days that Oostburg Bank would bail them out. They'd known for two days that Ted and Schneider would deliver a potent one-two punch today. Even so, after being beaten down for so long, landing a few blows of their own had felt mighty good. Since March, when Wolf's regional bank assigned their loan to HMR, they'd lived lives of constant worry. At the end of August, when HMR's pay-in-30-days ultimatum arrived, the worry escalated to terror. It'd been quite a reversal of fortune, all occurring in less than a month.

✳ ✳ ✳

After the call, Overdrive returned to his chopper and the bone-chilling wind and cold. Ever since the loan approval, he'd been trying to concentrate on next moves, without much luck. Deep down, he still feared Wolf and HMR. During the ensuing restless nights, he'd experienced a variety of nightmares all having the same theme ... Wolf destroying the family farm. These negative thoughts had been staying with him during the daytime, derailing his ability to think. All that changed with Ted's call. Suddenly, everything had clicked back into place. Overdrive may be cold and miserable, but his powers of concentration had returned. Bouncing along on the chopper, he found himself back in the flowing, creative mind-state where his best thinking was done.

Overdrive wanted the farm to stay in the family, and intended to do everything in his power to make that happen. He knew cajoling one of his kids to give farming a try would be a hell of a challenge. Opportunities elsewhere were becoming more attractive every year ... good incomes, regular hours, paid vacations, insurance, and retirement benefits. Compared with that, being your own boss, and having an active, healthy, outdoor lifestyle surrounded by the natural beauty of rural Wisconsin, wouldn't necessarily win the day. If to farm, meant a life of constant struggle to make ends meet, the kids wouldn't be interested and who could blame them. The farm had to be profitable enough to provide a good livelihood. He and Mary had doubled the milk production, but was that enough?

The more Overdrive thought about it, the more convinced he became that one major problem remained. If the price paid to dairy farmers for raw milk dropped, everything he and Mary had worked for could still unravel. Other businesses could set their prices based on cost plus a reasonable profit, but not farmers. Like it or not, farmers were expected to take what they're given, and somehow make do. It wasn't right.

Overdrive had been following in the farm magazines, the emergence of a new organization called the National Farmers Organization, or NFO. Among other things, the NFO hoped to prevent raw milk prices from tumbling. Overdrive decided the time was right to learn everything he could about the NFO. If it's legitimate, he'd discuss with Mary whether they should join.

Mind made up, Overdrive took a few slow deep breaths, and waited for the warm glow he usually felt after making a well-reasoned decision. Unfortunately, the warm glow never came. Instead, a deep sense of foreboding came over him. Was this merely a reaction to the foul weather? He hoped so, but feared not. The thought crossed his mind that today's events might have unintended consequences. As the wind gusted and howled anew, he hunched lower in the tractor seat, and tried to purge that negative thought.

CHAPTER 4

Rachel's Private Life – Thursday;
September 17, 1964; 12:00 Noon

Rachel Wolf sat in the kitchen nook of her Fond du Lac mansion, having lunch with her toddler son, Jake, and nanny, Rose. Jake had finished and was beginning to get antsy. Less than thrilled about mommy going away again, Jake demanded, "Mommy no go."

Rachel smiled and said, "I'm sorry sweetie, but mommy has to go. But it's only for a little while. When you wake up tomorrow, I'll be back."

Not mollified, Jake muttered, "Poopie-head!"

Rose left her seat, crouched to Jake's eye level, and said softly, "Jake, look at me." When he did, she continued, "Is that how we talk to mommy?"

Jake fidgeted, looked down, and then said in a tiny voice, "No."

Rose raised Jake's chin with a gentle caress, and then asked, "Now, what do we say?"

Jake held Rose's eyes, then looked to Rachel, and said, "Sorry, mommy."

Rachel smiled, and in a warm and encouraging voice, said, "Thank you, I accept your apology. You're such a big boy. Did you know only big boys know how to apologize?"

Jake giggled, and put his arms up, "I big!"

Rachel stepped over, swept Jake into her arms, and whispered into his ear, "Yes you are, Jake. You're a big boy."

Rose let mother and son enjoy the moment. But when the golden-blond mop-top began to get cranky, she said, "Hey, big boy, are you ready to go to your play room?"

Jake lit up, "Play room!"

Rachel gave one last squeeze, kissed both his cheeks, and said, "Jake, you be good for Rose. Mommy loves you. I'll see you in the morning." Then, she passed him to Rose, who carried him into the other room.

About then, the limo driver knocked and Rachel answered, "Ready when you are, Miss Wolf, I've got your bags. There's some road construction going north, so it might take three hours instead of two and a half."

Rachel nodded, "Thanks Brian, I'll be out shortly."

Rachel looked at her watch as Brian left. When Rose returned, Rachel pushed her up against the wall, and whispered, "How'd you like to give me a little something to tide me over? I may have to stay overnight."

They locked eyes, and soon Rose warmed, flushed, and began to pant. As she arched her back and lolled her head back, Rachel kissed her neck and nibbled her ears. Then Rachel began to French her deeply, while running her hands everywhere. Rose pulled up her sun dress and hooked one of her long shapely legs around Rachel's hip. Always commando at Rachel's insistence, Rose shuddered as Rachel's hand followed the line of her inner thigh upward, and penetrated the moistness beyond. Rose groaned and began to undulate. Then suddenly Rachel withdrew, gathered her coat and briefcase, and sashayed to the door. On her way out, Rachel tossed a randy glance at Rose, held it a moment, and then was gone.

* * *

For over a year, Rachel had busied herself pulling strings all over the State of Wisconsin, and the rewards for her efforts were finally coming to fruition. Her goal was to create a new reservation in partnership with the Potawatomi, and develop a casino there. Tonight's the tribal council meeting, and she's on the agenda to pitch the headwaters of the Milwaukee River, as the site for the casino. If approved, tomorrow she'll begin preparations for two state-agency approval-meetings in Madison, and lock down dates for them in late October. During the limo ride from Fond du Lac to Wabeno, she memorized her presentation.

Rachel's first order of business in the Wabeno area, was to rendezvous with her director of special projects, Vince Alder. Vince played no part in her legitimate businesses, but was second in command for swindles. Vince's big brother, "Milwaukee Phil" Alderisio, was a wise guy that ran prostitution, gambling, narcotics and loansharking in Milwaukee for the Chicago mob. When Phil and Vince were still kids in Chicago, Vince made a mistake and got on the wrong side of the Chicago bosses. To protect his brother, Phil sent Vince north to Wisconsin, helped him legally change his name to Alder, and advised him to assume a lower-profile and less-dangerous life of crime.

Over the years, Phil rose through the ranks, and eventually the Chicago bosses tasked him to extend the mob's reach to Milwaukee. When staffing his operation, Phil carefully selected people that didn't know he had a brother. Crime is a small world in Wisconsin, so Phil and Rachel Wolf soon crossed paths. He introduced her to Vince, and she took him on. In their first private conversation, Rachel told Vince she'd sig the Chicago mob on him if he ever crossed her. He's been a loyal and trusted lieutenant ever since.

On occasion, Rachel found Vince's bona fides with Phil to come in handy. When special projects came along that exceeded Vince's in-house capacity for dirty-work, extra resources could be tapped through Phil, no questions asked. As Vince liked to say, the bench was very deep. From day one, Rachel made it clear that Vince served at her pleasure. Only later did he realize what all that entailed. For example, when the boss was in the mood, servicing her with a smile was part of the job description. If the stability of their relationship served as any guide, both viewed the arrangement as win-win.

Brian guided the limo west from Wabeno, on County Hwy W, to the Wild Violet Pub & Grill on Roberts Lake. Rachel enjoyed the view there, and it's a place where she and Vince could talk privately, without fear of prying tribal eyes and ears. When Brian arrived, Vince's black Dodge 880 was already in the parking lot. Brian pulled the limo alongside, parked, and jumped out to open Rachel's door as Vince exited his car.

Vince and Brian both nodded, and Vince turned to Rachel, "Miss Wolf, so good to see you again."

Rachel offered a business-like smile, and said, "Likewise, I'm sure. Brian, please wait for us here. Vince and I need to speak privately inside."

Brian nodded, "As you wish, Miss Wolf."

Rachel headed inside, and Vince fell in beside her. Once settled, and after the drinks were ordered, Rachel said, "I'm ready. The prospectus is spot on, and I've figured a way to pitch it without getting lost in the weeds. I'd be shocked if the site isn't approved tonight."

Vince put his elbows on the table, and leaned in, "I'd be shocked to hear anything different from you."

Rachel kept her expression flat, "Well, well. I never know which Vince is going to show up. I guess tonight it's Mr. Smooth. That must mean you're no longer fretting over tonight's security plan."

Before Vince could answer, the drinks arrived and they ordered steak sandwiches and fries. Ever thoughtful, Rachel asked the waitress to take an order from the guy in the limo, and put it on her tab. Once alone, Vince said, "Council Hall holds about 500, and the elders expect standing room only. You'll be the center of attention, so I decided to go with overwhelming force. We'll be able to get you out of there unharmed, no matter what. In addition to me, there's 12 more men, and six more Dodge 880's. We can out-run and out-flank anybody. They're all carrying radios, and armed to the teeth with live ammo."

Rachel's eyebrows went up, "I appreciate your concern, Vince, but isn't that a little overkill? I'm going to lead the Potawatomi out of poverty. Why on earth would they go after me?"

Vince shook his head, "There's been a lot of violence up here lately, between whites and the tribe. Sure, it's mostly over fish and game. But in my experience, once people become comfortable with violence, it becomes the solution to all their problems."

Rachel stared at him a moment, then said, "You should know, I guess." After a pause, she continued, "Look, since we've got all these bodies up here anyway, let's put them to good use. They can pass out the prospectus and presentation hardcopies. I've got 600 each, in the trunk of the limo."

Vince nodded, "Sounds like a plan."

The food arrived, and they enjoyed the lake view while dining in silence. After finishing, Rachel cleared her throat, and said, "One more thing. If we get approval at the meeting, I'm going back to Fondy tonight. That way, tomorrow I can start cracking the whip on prep for the Madison meetings. But just in case something goes wrong, I've booked adjacent rooms for us at the Crandon Inn."

Vince's eyebrows went up, "I see. Hmm … what about the security detail? I mean, if something does go wrong, we'll need them to stay over."

Rachel chewed on her lower lip, then said, "Book them into that dive in Wabeno, just in case. We'll cancel everything if the approval comes through. And you …" She smiled and pointed a finger at him, "I swear, if you screw something up on purpose, just to force me to stay overnight, you'll regret it."

＊ ＊ ＊

Vince and Brian drove caravan-style from Roberts Lake to the tribal council venue in Wabeno. They arrived in plenty of time, and Rachel and the two men walked inside where they were greeted by Long Body, the chairman of tribal council. Long Body first met Rachel when he'd inquired about the prospects of a tribal loan at Fond du Lac regional bank. Although the bank had declined, Rachel's honest explanation had stuck with him. Later, she'd been appointed to the Wisconsin Conservation Commission's committee, responsible for investigating sportsmen-tribal tensions over fish and game. Rachel was the first to see poverty as the underlying problem. Long Body found it endearing, when she led the charge to legalize gaming on tribal lands, as the solution. By the time this idea became law, they'd become fast friends.

Long Body smiled broadly at Rachel, and said, "*Bozho, ni je na, nikan?* Hello, how are you, my friend?"

Rachel matched his smile, and said, "I'm well, Long Body, very well indeed." Then, she palmed her forehead and shook her head, "I'm sorry, I've already forgotten how to reply in your language."

Long Body fixed her with an empathetic gaze, "Well, even children of the tribe have such lapses, so don't feel bad. In their case, I'm obligated to scold because we're trying to keep our language alive. But for you, all is forgiven."

Rachel laughed, "Thank you, thank you. Say, you're probably wondering who these gentlemen are. Brian here, is my driver. Tonight, he'll also be setting up and taking down my screen and overhead projector. Vince here, manages things for me. Tonight, he and his team will distribute handouts and whatnot. In a hall this size, only the folks up front will be able to see the screen. I thought it'd be best if everybody had a copy of the prospectus and presentation."

Long Body offered a firm handshake to each man, and said, "Pleased to meet you both. Rachel, I'm impressed as always, with how well prepared you are.

While your guys get to work, how about I introduce you to the elders?"

Rachel nodded, "That'd be wonderful." Then, while walking off, she winked at Vince and Brian over her shoulder, and said, "Let's meet at the cars just before start time, to verify everything's set."

After hobnobbing with the tribal brass for about a half hour, Rachel stepped outside and into a circle with Vince and Brian, "Okay, tell me the plan."

Vince found her eyes, "There're four entrances but two additional exits, for a total of six. While the crowd is filtering in, we'll have two guys at each entrance and two pairs of rovers, all watching closely. Each pair will have enough handouts for the rows assigned to them. When the crowd is settled and handouts distributed, each pair stations at their assigned exit. If there's anything suspicious, they'll radio me, and I'll decide what to do from there."

Rachel nodded, "Okay, say there's a true threat. Then what?"

Vince, now grim, "Minor things we'll just handle. Monitor people, maybe ask them to leave, or whatnot. But if the problem expands and I'm not sure we can contain it, we're out of here. In that event, I'll radio Brian to start the cars and open the doors, you and I will run to Brian, and the other guys will block all the exits or die trying." Pointing now, Vince continued, "The cars are right there, outside the exit nearest the stage. If we run, the guys stationed there will cover our retreat. I'll lead with the muscle car, and you'll get in the limo with Brian. Once on the move, I'll call in the other six cars. Any resistance encountered will be crushed. At no time will the limo be left unprotected. We'll all be in radio contact the whole time. There'll be me and two other cars ahead of the limo and four cars behind. The primary destination is Fond du Lac, but if that escape route is compromised, the secondary is your Wolf's Run estate. Either way, the limo has a seven-car escort and 13 guns between you and harm's way. 14 counting Brian."

Rachel nodded again, "Okay, I got it. Now say there's a true threat. How'll I even know."

Vince lowered his voice and leaned in, "During your remarks, you usually like to roam the stage. Do that, and regularly glance in my direction. I'll be stationed stage left, along the outside wall, and under a light so you can see my face. You'll have a direct line of sight. Always hold your glance long enough for me to look your way. If there's a true threat I'll wink, otherwise I'll nod. At the sight of a wink, roam left immediately and I'll come for you."

Rachel admired him for a moment, "You love this shit, don't you?"

Through a predatory grin, Vince said lightly, "Almost better that sex."

CHAPTER 5

Rachel Makes Her Pitch – Thursday;
September 17, 1964; 6:45 PM

Potawatomi Tribal Council Hall was abuzz, when Long Body strolled to the microphone and cleared his throat to silence the room. He briefly reviewed the agenda, then launched into an overview of the tribe's partnership with Development Partners LLC and its purpose. The hall's atmosphere turned electric when he disclosed that DP was here tonight, seeking approval for a specific location for the new reservation and casino.

After Long Body's introduction, Rachel strode confidently onto the stage, smiling broadly and making eye contact with members of the audience, near and far. After the thankyou's, she instantly put everyone at ease by joking that anyone sitting beyond row 10, eagle-eyed or not, wouldn't be able to see a thing SO SHE BROUGHT HANDOUTS! As Vince's men distributed copies of the prospectus and presentation, she asked the tribe's A/V assistant to put up the first overhead, a map of Wisconsin and adjoining states. Then, while referencing the map, she launched into a colorful, entertaining, and thoroughly convincing opening argument on why the Headwaters of the Milwaukee River was the ideal location. Artfully planted within, were the key points of her argument, which she'd return to during her full remarks.

With the crowd resettled, handouts in hand, Rachel began in earnest. Relaxed and roaming the dais with her mic, she smiled as she spoke, and made eye contact all over the room. She maintained a modest speaking tempo so everyone could follow along. For those reliant on handouts, she made references to page, figure, and table numbers, and paused long enough for her audience to find them. She included Vince in every visual rotation to the crowd, and always made certain to linger there long enough for him to notice. Eloquent and with a compelling story, the rapt silence told Rachel she had the audience's full attention.

Everything went like clockwork during the presentation. There'd been no winks from Vince, although he and Rachel both noticed a man in the second row snapping photos and running a tape recorder. Through eye contact and slight head motions, Rachel directed Vince to find out who that was. She knew he understood, when he pulled his radio and alerted the team. Shortly after, she noticed one of Vince's guys whispering with a tribal policeman, while pointing toward the man. Satisfied, Rachel refocused on the crowd. People were hanging on every word, and more and more of them were nodding subconsciously. Always a good sign. When she finished, the hall exploded in loud applause.

Afterward, tribal members were given the opportunity to ask questions and voice their yeah or nay positions. As Long Body had explained to Rachel earlier, only council members had actual votes. But before casting their ballots, the elders wanted to know where the tribe in general, and specifically their own band, stood. Rachel remained on stage during this period, but few questions came her way so she drifted to Vince's side of the hall. The overwhelming sentiment of the crowd was to move forward. But toward the end, to Rachel's surprise, several tribal members voiced strong opposition. They felt building a casino on sacred lands with burial mounds would dishonor their ancestors. She motioned Vince over, and whispered for him to identify the naysayers.

After everyone had said their peace, council voted to approve, with one dissenting vote. As Long Body thanked everyone and adjourned the meeting, Rachel noticed Vince coming back her way, and stepped down into the aisle to meet him privately.

Vince slowed as he approached, and said in a low voice, "The guy in the second row goes by the name of Darkwater Flint. The two opposers go by Round Wind and Cedar Root. All three are from the Little Prairie Band, and the band's elder, Make Wit, was the lone dissenting vote."

Rachel frowned, "Huh. Flint doesn't sound as native as the others."

Vince nodded, "That's the interesting part. He's a half breed that regularly visits his white relatives near Waldo, down in Sheboygan County."

Rachel's eyebrows shot up, "Oh-oh."

Vince bobbed his head, "It gets worse. He's also friends with a retired farmer from Cascade. A guy by the name of Old Bill Evans. Apparently, Old Bill used to own the band's sacred lands."

Rachel's eyes narrowed, "Evans, oh shit!" She thought a moment, "Old Bill must be James Evans's father. The casino site covers four parcels, one being the Evans farm, which I don't officially own until the end of the month. We can't let those snapshots, tapes, and handouts get to Cascade, or I may never own it. Follow Flint, but be careful not to spook him."

Vince jerked a look, "The crowd's already moving, and he's in it."

Rachel, "Go, go, go! Come back when it's under control. I'll either be hobnobbing with the elders, or waiting in the limo with Brian."

* * *

The elders hung around for a good half hour after the meeting adjourned, and Rachel worked the crowd with gusto. She cornered Long Body, and asked, "What can you tell me about the Little Prairie Band?"

Long Body's eyebrows went up, "You have your sources, I see. Little Prairie is one of the smaller bands in the tribe and has roots, including burial mounds, somewhere on the lands we're calling the Headwaters of the Milwaukee River."

Contrite, Rachel said, "There're sacred lands at the site? I didn't know that. Could you introduce me to Little Prairie's elder? I'd like to reassure him, if I can."

Long Body smiled and nodded, "That's an excellent idea. Let me see ..." He scanned the hall, then said, "There he is. Follow me."

After introducing Rachel to Make Wit, Long Body left to give them some privacy. Rachel said, "Make Wit, I'm glad we have this chance to talk. Until just now, I had no idea there were Little Prairie Band burial mounds on the site. I can guarantee you that we'll never, ever, disturb those mounds, or desecrated your sacred lands in any way."

Somewhat standoffish, Make Wit said, "Reassurances along those lines are very welcome, Miss Wolf, but I'm afraid we've heard them before."

Rachel touched him on the forearm, "Please, call me Rachel."

Make Wit nodded, "Alright, Rachel then. But just so you know, ever since the Headwaters of the Milwaukee River came under consideration, we of the Little Prairie Band have lived with heavy hearts. Those lands are in our thoughts daily. Many of us still remember times past, when we pilgrimaged there. Each spring, the headwaters ran dark with giant pike in spawn. We feasted on them, and offered them ceremonially to our ancestors."

Rachel, genuinely intrigued, "Interesting, you actually participated in these pilgrimages in your lifetime? So, they continued until fairly recently, then?"

Make Wit nodded thoughtfully, "Well, they ended in the mid-1920s. But it's amazing how brightly the memories still burn after 40 years."

Rachel offered a smile, "If you don't mind my asking, why did they stop?"

Make Wit, now grim, "Increasingly, mother earth became marred by fence lines, roads, and railroad tracks, and populated by people intolerant of our beliefs. But to their credit, the Evans family always welcomed us with great warmth." He paused, and smiled at the memory, "They stocked our traditional encampment with split wood before we arrived, and were genuinely happy to see us. Under their stewardship, the sacred lands remained in their natural state." Then, Make Wit's face darkened, "But eventually, the hostility endured during the journey could no longer be offset by the spiritual renewal gained. It just wasn't worth it anymore."

Rachel seemed moved, "I'm so sorry to hear that, and thank you for explaining. This helps me understand the passionate objections raised during council. By Round Wind and Cedar Root, was it?"

Make Wit's mood lightened, "Yes, of course. Round Wind, aptly named for what's commonly known among your people as a tornado. Always best to stay out of his path. And Cedar Root, strong like the wood that refuses to turn to dust. None are more steadfastly wedded to tradition than he. I hope you understand they meant no disrespect. Every band would've spoken out in defense of their sacred lands."

Rachel nodded, "I do understand. Of course, I do." Confident she'd established rapport, she probed further, "Just out of curiosity, does the name Darkwater Flint ring a bell?"

Make Wit bobbed his head, "Yes, of course." He chuckled, "You might say Darkwater's a living example of renewal from a pilgrimage. One year while at the Evans farm, a young woman of ours met and became inseparable from one of the Flint boys, who lived nearby. Darkwater was the result. Why do you ask?"

Rachel smiled, "I'm just trying to understand the depth of your band's passion for the Headwaters of the Milwaukee River. I'd overheard from someone here, that Darkwater had a special connection to the place."

Make Wit looked at her, reevaluating, "He does indeed. So, tell me more about your tidings of reassurance."

Rachel instantly dialed up the charm, and told Make Wit exactly what she knew he wanted to hear. She'd wanted to learn more about Darkwater, but felt she'd pushed it as far as she dared. As the conversation petered out, Rachel saw Vince approaching, and excused herself.

Rachel moved to an isolated spot in the hall, and waited as Vince came to her. Walking fast, Vince slowed as he came up, and said in a low voice, "I put a tail on Flint. But they radioed back for advice, when he started doing evasive maneuvers. I told them to break it off, rather than be made."

Rachel's eyebrows went up, "Huh. Do you think he's a pro?"

Vince shook his head, "Shouldn't be, at least based on what we know. We've been asking a lot of questions among tribal police and members of the tribe. They say he's a hunting and fishing guide up in Eagle River."

Rachel scowled, "Well, I need him found. What's the plan?"

With assurance, Vince said, "Doing evasive maneuvers suggests he's spooked. We know his address but rather than grab him now, it'd be better to give him some time to relax and let his guard down. From the sounds of it, the whole tribe is out celebrating. I figure Flint will do the same, once he gets over the jitters. We know his car, so the team is out looking for it at all the shit-hole bars around here, as we speak. If we find it, we'll sit on it and grab him there. If he hasn't turned up by the time the bars thin out, we'll get him at his house, later."

Rachel looked disappointed in him, "Vince, we don't want Flint. We want the snapshots, tapes, and handouts. If you find the car at a bar, for Christ's sake search it!" She thought a moment, "In fact, why not look in on the house now? If the car is gone, search it. If not, we'll need to deliberate on our next step. In that case, do a thorough reconnaissance of the place, so we know what our options are. I'll be in the limo after the elders clear out, you can reach me on Brian's radio."

* * *

Rachel stayed at the hall until the last elder left, and then Brian drove her to a diner for a late-night snack. Afterward, he drove to an open park-like area in Wabeno, where Rachel could enjoy a nice view of the moonlit landscape. Vince checked-in frequently by radio, each time darkening her mood. There'd been no sign of Flint's car at the bars, but when they checked the house, they found it there. The most recent updates concerned recon around the house. Her impatience grew as the hour swung past midnight. When the radio squawked again, Rachel barked, "Goddammit Vince, we've wasted enough time. I'm ready to make a decision."

Vince hesitated, then said, "Sometimes these radios aren't as secure as you'd think. Where are you? I'll come to you." Rachel told him, and five minutes later Vince pulled up behind the limo.

As Vince settled into the back seat, Rachel said, "Give me the latest."

Vince sucked in a breath, and talked fast, "The car was unlocked, and there's nothing in it. The house lights are out, so he's probably sleeping. But the shades are pulled in the bedroom, so we can't be sure. A few of the other windows were uncovered, but we couldn't really see anything in the dark. The bedroom window and one other have screens, and are open. But the doors are locked."

Rachel wrinkled her brow, "Huh. It'd be pretty easy to get in a window."

Vince, shook his head, "Well, not really. The street's a dead end, and Flint's house is the last one on the left. The last lot on the right has nothing but a foundation covered in rubble from a fire. But there're other houses, next door, across from that, and several more on down. They're all occupied and really close together. This time of year, just like Flint, they're sleeping with their windows open. I doubt we'd be able to break in without Flint or a neighbor hearing."

Rachel nodded, "Okay. Tell me about the house."

Vince thought a moment, then said, "The house looks like a dilapidated shit-hole. They all do. Probably built around the turn of the century. All-wood, not much paint left. When I tried Flint's doors, every floor board on both porches creaked. I'll bet every door hinge squeaks and window sticks. It's hard to believe we'd get in without being heard. Flint will probably be armed. Hell, everybody up here is. The last thing we need is a shootout."

Rachel held a hand to her forehead as she thought a moment, "It's the last house on a dead end, right? What's on the back side?"

Vince's eyes narrowed, "Woods, mostly, and beyond that another road with no houses nearby."

Rachel sat up taller, "Would it be possible to park on the next road over, and reach the house undetected by going cross lots through the woods?"

Vince shrugged, "Sure, but so what? We can get to the house from the street. The problem is, what to do when we get there?"

Rachel ignored his response, "How far is the car

from the house?"

Uncertain where her mind was headed, Vince said, "It's nosed in aside the house on the right, maybe only a foot away, but stopped short so the driver's door can open. It looks like he parks there to be under the overhanging eave. If it's raining, he can get into the house without getting wet."

Rachel came to a snap decision, "Go in the back way, and torch both the house and car. With the car parked so close, the fire marshal will think it started in the house, and spread to the car."

Startled, Vince jerked and hit his head on the door post, "Are you sure?"

Rachel darkened, "Why wouldn't I be? Accidents happen all the time, right? Hell, there's a burnt pile of rubble right across the street, so it's not even uncommon in the neighborhood. Like you say, it's a poorly maintained shit hole. Looks like too much DIY wiring to me."

Flabbergasted, Vince asked, "But what if Flint doesn't get out?"

A predatory smile spread across Rachel's lips, "Even better. But make sure you light up that car, too. If he does manage to escape the house with the goods, we don't want him to have wheels. Call me in Fondy in the morning, Brian's driving me back tonight."

CHAPTER 6

Manhunt by Team Rachel – Friday;
September 18, 1964; 2:00 AM

B rian attacked the empty pre-dawn roads between Wabeno and Fond du Lac with a lead foot. Rachel managed to doze off a few times, but with so much on her mind, the spells weren't restful. By the time they reached home, it's the wee hours of the following day. Upon arrival, she told Brian the bags could wait until morning. Then she let herself in, slipped out of her shoes, and tiptoed to her bedroom. In a daze, she left a trail of clothes on the way to the bathroom. After a quick pee and a brush and rinse of her teeth, a naked Rachel slipped into bed. Once horizontal, she was out. A moment later, Rose crept through the door from the adjoining bedroom, and spooned in behind her.

Neither moved until the phone rang at 6:30 AM. Groggy, Rachel rolled over for the handset, discovered Vince on the line, and asked Rose to go make some coffee. Once she'd gone, Rachel hissed, "This better be important."

Vince exhaled heavily, "It's important all right.

There's no body."

Rachel swung her legs out of bed and jerked to a sitting position, "W-what?"

Steeling himself for what was to come, Vince repeated, "There's no body at the scene of the fire."

Rachel barked, "How's that even possible?"

Vince, struggling to stay calm, "We had the place surrounded on all sides, and he didn't come out. He must've never been there."

Rachel snapped, "But his car!"

Vince muttered, "He must've dropped the car, and hitched a ride with someone else. Not sure why he stayed out overnight. Maybe he's at a friend's house, passed out drunk. If he went out partying with the rest of the tribe, I doubt he took the goods with him. If he left them behind, they're toast now."

Rachel scoffed, "We can't assume that. We need to know for sure. Find out who picked him up, and where he's at now."

After ruminating a moment, Vince said, "Okay, the neighbors will be rolling out of bed soon. How about I have my team canvas them. Somebody must've seen who picked him up. We've no authority or standing around here, so we'll have to be careful and discrete ..."

Rachel interrupted, "Your goons and *careful and discrete* should never be mentioned in the same sentence. I'll call Long Body. Maybe I can get him to direct tribal police to help out. Hold off until I get back to you."

Vince, after a moment of empty air, "But why would he do that?"

Rachel said wisely, "The tribe is destitute, and he wants that casino as much as I do. Once he learns Flint possesses information that might screw up the whole deal, he'll sic the tribal police after him. Trust me."

Vince thought about that, then said, "Maybe so, but he'll need a story. He just helped you sell the tribe on the HMR site. He wouldn't want word getting around that you don't even own all the property yet."

Rachel groaned, "Good point." She shook her head, then said, "Look, I haven't had my coffee yet, and nothing's coming to me. After the caffeine kicks in, I'll concoct something and call Long Body. He'll need to tell his police chief how to reach you. Where're you calling from?"

Vince admitted, "I'm on the pay phone outside the Wabeno Diner, and plan to have breakfast when we're done. They can reach me here, or tune to my team's radio frequency." Vince gave her that, then hung up.

❋ ❋ ❋

Rachel tidied up and put on pajamas and a robe, before stepping into her slippers and heading down to the kitchen. There, she's greeted by Rose's radiant smile, plus the aroma of freshly ground coffee, and a breakfast casserole hot out of the oven. Beat and famished, she allowed herself to be waited on, hand and foot.

After a respectful period of time, Rose asked, "Is everything okay?"

Rachel shook off Rose's concern, "Oh sure, it'll be fine." Then, she changed the subject, "But the damn phone pulled me up from a wonderful deep sleep."

Rose mimed indignation of her own, "Yes seriously, I just hate it when that happens. I hope it was important."

"It was," but Rachel didn't elaborate. Instead, she rubbed her stomach, "Rose, this casserole is to die for! It's just what I needed, thank you. Can I have a little more coffee, please?"

"Of course!" Rose wrinkled her nose in delight, and hopped up to get the pot. After pouring another cup, she asked, "Can I get you anything else?"

Without saying a word, Rachel let her gaze, or leer to be more exact, linger on her so-called nanny. Rose blushed and giggled, to which Rachel responded, "That'll have to wait until later. Duty calls. I'll be in the study, mostly on the phone. When Jake wakes up, bring him in to see me."

* * *

Rachel created a storyline to hook Long Body over breakfast, and reran it through her mind a few times in the study, before calling him at 7:30 AM. When he picked up, she said perkily, "Top of the morning to you, Long Body. I'm so sorry to disturb you at this rude hour."

Long Body laughed, "Oh, you needn't worry, Rachel. I'm an early riser, always have been."

Cheerfully, Rachel said, "That's good to know. I'm afraid the same can't be said for me. Look, we have a situation and I need your help."

After a silent pause, Long Body said, "I'm listening."

Contrite, Rachel said, "It's quite embarrassing, actually. I'm afraid anticipation for the day when we'd break ground together on the casino, has caused me a slight lapse in judgement. I wanted us onsite with dozers as soon as next spring's thaw allowed, so I built the rest of the casino-plan's schedule around that assumption. Then according to that, our proposal needed to be before the two state agencies by the end of October. This was only possible if the tribe's approval of the site was secured at last night's meeting."

Long Body interrupted, "I'm confused. We did secure approval last night."

Rachel exhaled heavily, "Well, here's the thing. The HMR site consists of four land parcels, and I don't actually own one of them until September 30th."

After a long pause, Long Body said, "I see." Then, choosing his words carefully, "But that's not what you told the tribe last night."

Rachel conceded, "No, it isn't, and I apologize for that. But getting into the weeds about parcels would've been confusing in front of such a large crowd. I chose to keep things simple. At the time, the risk of not controlling all the land by month's end was miniscule. Unfortunately, that's no longer the case."

Long Body, not bothering to hide his anger, "Well, why the hell not? Goddammit Rachel, I put my reputation on the line to get that approval!"

In a soft, reassuring tone, Rachel said, "I know you did. Just relax, okay? Everything's going to be fine, if we stay on the same page. That last parcel is the Evans farm. You know, the one with the Little Prairie Band's burial mounds. As it turns out, a band member is friends with the Evans family, and he left last night's meeting with photos, audio tape and the handouts. As you recall, two band members also spoke in opposition to the deal, and their elder voted against it. None of this is a coincidence. Little Prairie is trying to kill the deal, and they just might succeed if Evans gets those meeting materials before that farm is mine. I, or rather we, can't allow that to happen."

Long Body exploded, "God damn sonofabitch! That fucking Little Prairie Band! No matter what I do, they're always trying to gum up the works. They've made being a squeaky wheel into a new art form, and I'm sick of it."

Elated by the unexpected outburst, Rachel played along, "Exactly. We need to stop them. Those materials can't reach Evans. Are you with me?"

Long Body sputtered, "You're damn right I am! What do you propose?"

Rachel pumped her fist, then confided carefully, "Before I get into that, I need to brief you on a few current events. The guy with the goods is named Darkwater Flint. Last night his house and car went up in flames."

Long Body gasped, "W-what?" But then after a beat, he said, "Wait a minute ... does that mean our problem is solved?"

Rachel asked, "Have you ever heard of plausible deniability?" After Long Body said yes, Rachel continued carefully, "Let's just say that unfortunately, we don't know for sure if the fire solved our problem. Flint wasn't there, and he may still have the goods."

Long Body sounded disappointed, "I see. So, going back to my original question, what do you propose?"

Rachel said, "We're trying to find Flint, and need your tribal police to help."

Long Body thought about that, then said, "Hmm ... I see. That's possible, I suppose, but it'd be awkward." After another pause, he said, "What would I tell the chief? I can't very well tell him the truth. And I can't risk word getting around that I'm playing favorites among the bands, either. I'd need a story."

Rachel admitted, "That's fair enough. Why not just tell him that Flint is wanted for questioning, concerning the fire that destroyed his property? Tell him the casino requires state approvals, and the first thing they'll look at is whether the tribe can maintain law and order. Tell him a birdy told you it looks like arson, and the last thing the tribe needs right now is an unsolved case of insurance fraud."

Long Body chewed on that for a moment, and finally said, "That'd work."

Rachel told Long Body how the chief could reach Vince, then said, "If anybody ever asks, DP will cooperate fully with the fire investigation."

* * *

Rachel was in the kitchen having another cup of coffee when Rose appeared, carrying the little man. Rachel cooed, "There's my big boy!"

Jake threw up his arms, and said, "I big, mommy!"

Rachel hopped off her stool and walked toward them with arms outstretched, "Yes, you are! Oh, yes you are!" Rose handed Jake over, and Rachel snuggled him onto a hip, kissed a chubby cheek, and asked, "How's my big boy today?"

Jake pressed his forehead to hers, and giggled, "Happy! Mommy home!"

Rachel touched noses with him, and said, "I'm happy, too, sweetie. Are you hungry?" After Jake's exaggerated head bob, she said, "That's my boy. Eating makes you big and strong. Where do we go to eat?"

Jake pursed his lips, pointed to the high chair, and said "Chair."

Rachel smiled and nodded, "That's right. Chair. High chair. You're growing so big. I hope you still fit." Rachel walked to the chair, and slid him in, "There you go. It looks like Rose has something for you."

Rose stepped near and dropped some Cheerios on Jake's tray to get him started. Just then the phone rang, and Rachel said, "I'll take that in the study. Jake, you be good for Rose."

Breathless after the quick jog, Rachel picked up to find Vince on the line. After the hellos, she said, "What's new?"

In a clipped, just-the-facts manner, Vince said, "The chief of tribal police reached me, and we're working together. He seems to think we're after Flint not the goods, but same difference at this point. One of Flint's neighbors told us his girlfriend picked him up last night, maybe an hour or so after council adjourned. Her name is Robin Thunder, and she lives in Laona, about eight miles north of Wabeno. My guys arrived there about 8:15 AM, and got her out of the shower. She wouldn't open the door for strangers, so we fetched a tribal squad car and covered all the exits until they arrived. Flint wasn't there and remarkably, this mystified Thunder. She claimed he'd been eating breakfast when she went into the shower. Half-eaten leftovers and a note saying *'thanks for last night'* seemed to support her story. He must've fled out the back door on foot when we arrived. Thunder didn't know anything. She hadn't attended tribal council. She said Flint had called her afterward, and invited her to go celebrate with the rest of the tribe. She drove, and they ended up at her place. Thunder did say he'd brought along a pack last night, with a change of clothes. The pack's gone, so he must've taken it with him."

Rachel pounded her desk, "God dammit!" Then snapped, "We should've cornered him at the house right after the meeting. Are you after him?"

In a confident tone, Vince said, "He's being tracked

on foot, and my team and tribal police have the whole area flooded. We should have him soon."

Rachel, in a frosty voice, "You'd better. And grab that pack when you do. Call me when you know more."

* * *

Though shaking with rage, Rachel managed to channel that energy to the task of spinning up a large team of lawyers and accountants to prepare for the state agency meetings. To stay on schedule, she needed those meetings in the rearview mirror by October's end. It took over a dozen calls, but by the time Rachel broke for lunch the '*suits*', as she called them, were finally rolling.

After lunch, the phone rang while Rachel was on her way back to the study. It was Vince with an update, "Tribal police trackers were following Flint on foot, but lost him. My team and more police have the surrounding roads covered, and he hasn't crossed them, so he couldn't have gone far. We think he's gone to ground within our search area. Now, the tribe's bringing in their canine trackers. They've got Flint's pillow case from Thunder's house, to use for scent."

Rachel snapped, "They should've brought in the dogs right away."

Vince conceded, "I agree. If I'd known they had dogs, I'd have insisted."

Rachel, voice still cold, "You should've known. Catch that asshole, Vince, and grab the pack before the police do. We don't want anybody beyond Long Body to know what we're really after. The police think this's an arsonist manhunt, and we need to keep it that way. Call again when you know more."

＊ ＊ ＊

Rachel spent the next several hours working the phones with her suits. The experience made her marvel at how bereft of reasoning skills, highly educated professional people were. After a late afternoon potty break, Rose caught Rachel red handed in the kitchen, looking for a snack.

Rose purred, "Jake's down for his nap. He's such a joy to be with."

Rachel smiled, "He is, isn't he? I just love that giggle when I wiggle my nose in his belly. I'd eat him right up, if I could."

Rose unfolded her arms, "How're you doing?"

Rachel shrugged, "Oh, I'm fine. A little tired, is all."

Rose stepped forward, and tucked a lock of Rachel's hair behind her ear, "I don't know, you seem a little tense to me. You sure there isn't something I should be doing, you know, to relieve all that tension?"

Rachel began to lean in, but jerked back when the phone rang. As she jogged toward the study, she shouted over her shoulder, "Hold that thought!"

Rachel broke into a dead run, worried she'd miss the call. Breathless, she grabbed the handset, and Vince was on the line. Less confident than before, he said, "The dogs picked up Flint's trail near where the original trackers lost him. Unfortunately, Flint's trail led across two roads and into the Chewamagon-Nicolet national forest. This never should've happened Rachel, I'm sorry. My team and tribal police were all over those roads but somehow, he slipped through. From where Flint entered, it's a long way to anywhere. Our problem now is the enormous search area. More trackers and dogs are on the way. We'll get him eventually, but it may take some time."

Not bothering to hide her anger, Rachel snapped, "You're all a bunch of idiots! How can a guy that looked to be in his mid-50's be so hard to catch?"

Contrite, Vince said, "Look, I said I'm sorry. I know you don't want to hear excuses, but Flint is half Potawatomi and wily as hell. He's been setting up diversions, one after the other. But don't worry, he'll never be able to evade the dogs. And the hunt will continue around the clock, until we get him."

Rachel, still frosty, "See that you do. And call me with anything important."

Rachel spent the rest of the day working the phones with her suits. Their conceptual uptake remained disappointingly slow, but progress was being made. Nonetheless, they still didn't fully grasp what she needed done, let alone how to do it. In fairness, they're working on the first project under a new legislative authority, and she guessed they'd probably have to break some new ground.

Dinner time with Rose and Jake was a true joy. The meal Rose prepared was delicious, and Jake said a new word. Afterward, Rose cleaned up while Rachel enjoyed some quality time with her son on the floor in the play room. Jake loved constructing things with his tinker toys. Just watching him reason through the assembly of pieces, and learning to exercise his motor skills, gave Rachel a tingle. Time stood still in the joy of the moment, and she couldn't believe it when Rose peaked in to say it's bed time. Where had all the time gone?

Jake's expanding vocabulary filled Rachel's heart with pride. Saying *bed time* flipped a switch, and yawns and sleepy eyes soon followed. When Rachel stood and bent over to pick him up, the tired little man raised his arms. Mother and child slowed as they approached Rose at the door, and Rachel whispered she'd put Jake to bed. Rose dropped a kiss atop Jake's head as he passed, and at the same time, caressed Rachel's backside. The women locked eyes for a moment, then Rose slowly turned and lithely swayed her hips as she walked down the hall. Caught hesitating to enjoy the view when Rose glanced back over her shoulder, Rachel made a face and stuck out her tongue, then took Jake to bed.

After Jake drifted off, Rachel and Rose spent some quality time under the covers until the phone rang at 10:00 PM. After a brief struggle to free herself from the jumble of tangled arms and legs, Rachel rolled over and knocked the handset to the floor by accident. Cursing, she retrieved it and hissed, "This better be good."

Contrite, Vince said, "Sorry to wake you, Rachel. I thought you'd still be up, and would sleep better with the news. Flint's scent led the dogs to a major east-west hiking trail in the national forest. Flint is headed west. The trackers have covered a lot of ground, so Flint's moving fast. I doubt the old guy can keep it up all night. If all goes well, we should have him by morning."

Rachel relaxed, and said, "Thanks Vince, I will sleep better. Call again when you know more. Don't worry about the time, this's important."

Rachel collapsed back into bed, snuggled up close to Rose, and instantly fell asleep. The next thing she knew, an irritating disturbance had entered her consciousness and wouldn't go away. Unable to ignore it any longer, she resurfaced to find the phone ringing, and lunged at it to stop that awful noise.

Through bleary-eyes, the clock read 5:10 AM as she exhaled a weak yes into the mouthpiece, and heard Vince say, "The dogs left the main trail following a fresh scent, leading uphill along a stream. The trackers thought for sure they had Flint cornered, but then the scent petered out. They tried all directions from where it ended, but found nothing. Then, on the way back downhill, one of the dogs was spotted with something in its mouth. It turned out to be a rag from a T-shirt. The trackers think Flint tore one up and planted the rags to create a diversion. Now they're back on the main trail heading west. Bottom line, they wasted some time, but the dogs are frothing so the scent is really fresh. Shouldn't be long now."

Rachel rubbed her eyes with her free hand, "Don't count your chickens just yet. Like you say, the geezer has skills. Keep me posted."

Still beyond tired, Rachel was no sooner horizontal than out. She dreamed that gratitude had physical form, and saw herself grinning from ear to ear, floating in an ocean of it. Comforted by the gentle swell and perfect weather, a carousel of life-affirming images flashed through her mind. But at some point, this state of eternal bliss was once again rudely interrupted. Barely discernible at the far reaches of her consciousness, was that same annoying disturbance. Each swell became stronger than the one before, until the last one jolted her awake.

Rose hissed, "Are you going to answer that, or what? I've been nudging you over and over. It's on about the sixth ring."

Startled, Rachel muttered, "Huh? Oh. What? Oh … yeah, I'll get it." The clock glowed 6:30 AM as she stretched for the handset. When Vince responded to her weak hello, she covered the mouthpiece and asked Rose to go make some coffee. Once alone, Rachel squeaked, "Okay, I'm here."

Deflated, Vince said, "Shortly after dawn, they thought they had Flint again. The dogs went wild, and pulled the trackers off the main trail, down along a stream, and around a bend behind a hill. There, they found a makeshift shelter and fire pit, still warm. They canvassed the area, but other than the path in, found no scent. Either he got into the stream and waded further into the wilderness, or he backtracked. Tired of Flint's bullshit, they split the dogs and searched both ways."

Rachel swung her legs out of bed, rotated her nakedness to a sitting position, then muttered, "It's about damn time they stopped underestimating Flint."

Vince wearily rattled on, "The group that went back to the main trail picked up Flint's scent again, heading west. They radioed, and the others hustled back to join them. It's a good thing because soon after, they came upon a three-way fork, and had to split up again. The big fear was Flint might head in one direction, only to bushwhack to another. They went a quarter mile down each route, and as it turned out, the only scent was still on the main trail headed west. They've regrouped and are hauling ass, as we speak."

Shivering, Rachel pulled covers around herself, "Flint must've shot out of that camp like a cannon ball. Any chance he abandoned the pack in the shelter?"

Vince pooh-poohed that idea, "They looked in the shelter and did a cursory search of the area, but came up empty. They didn't want to waste a lot of time on it because, you know, there's probably a million places to ditch a pack out there."

Rachel, fog slowly clearing, "Any idea where the main trail goes?"

Vince sighed, "Crandon, eventually. By straight-arrow road, that's about 12 miles west of Laona. Counting the trek from Thunder's house to the national forest, and the winding trails once there, Flint will've covered over 20 miles if he makes Crandon. Don't laugh, he's within hailing distance. The trackers have radioed ahead, and a tribal police mobile unit is sitting on the trail head."

Fatigued, Rachel muttered, "It just gets better and better, doesn't it? We've got a serious problem if he gets to Crandon. He could steal a car, or borrow one from a friend. He'll be in the wind in no time."

Vince exhaled, "Man, I'm so punch drunk I hadn't even thought of that."

Rachel's mind raced, "Are we absolutely certain we're tracking Flint? Him making 20 miles over rough terrain seems unbelievable. I mean, what if he handed a few dirty T-shirts to some twenty-something Little Prairie asshole."

Vince muttered, "Well, if that happened, we're screwed." He ruminated a moment, then said, "But I don't believe it did. When my guys and tribal police arrived at Thunder's house, Flint had just fled on foot. Hell, his coffee was still warm. And we've been close on his tail ever since. It's hard to believe he had a twenty-something stashed in the woods behind Thunder's house."

Mollified, Rachel said, "Okay, so it's Flint, and he may make Crandon. That means Crandon's the new search area, and you and the tribal police need to throw everything you've got in that direction. The chief will probably need to hear that from Long Body, so I'll call him and make that happen. Need anything else?"

Vince replied unwisely, "A little sleep would be nice."

Rachel snapped, "Listen up, Vince. Be careful what you wish for. Bring me Flint's pack, or a restful eternity may be yours sooner than you think."

* * *

Now fully awake, Rachel stepped into the bathroom to do her business and clean up. After splashing her face and patting dry, Rachel felt refreshed, and headed to the kitchen. There, on a stool at the kitchen island, sat Rose head in hands, and drooped over her half-empty coffee cup. Afraid she'd startle, Rachel softly sang a few bars of *Can't Buy Me Love* as she poured herself some java. After Rose stirred, she stepped over to caress her back.

Rose leaned back into her, and Rachel whispered, "Hey, gorgeous. You don't seem to be your perky self this morning."

Through an exaggerated pout, Rose stuck out her tongue, then said, "Hard to be perky after a night like that." Then she mimed being deep in thought, "Let me guess. You can't talk about whatever's going on, right?"

Rachel tilted her head, caught Rose's eye, and said, "I'm afraid I can't."

Rose offered her a tiny smile, "Okay, I won't ask." She sipped her coffee, then asked, "How about some breakfast?"

Rachel smiled, "That's a great idea."

After breakfast, Rachel went to the study and called Long Body. After filling him in, she got right to the point, "The way things are going, Flint will make it to Crandon. Once there, he's only a borrowed or stolen car away from disappearing. I've sent all my people in that direction. Can you do any more on your end?"

More to himself, Long Body said, "Well ... let's see." Then after a moment, he suggested, "I could call the chief of tribal police, and tell him we need all-hands in Crandon, and suggest he request backup from the Forest County Sherriff's department. Chief and the Sherriff back each other up all the time, so it wouldn't raise eyebrows. He could say he needed help to apprehend an arsonist on the run."

Rachel, in a grateful tone, "Sounds like a plan. Your chief knows how to reach my Vince. Those two and the Sherriff probably ought to meet in person. Crandon's a lot bigger than Laona. They'll need to get their act together."

* * *

Rachel spent most of the day riding the phones with her lawyers and accountants, but managed to work in some quality time with Jake between naps. The phone rang at 6:00 PM, just as she sat down to dinner. Apologizing profusely, Rachel asked Rose to keep a plate warm, and ran to the study to pick up the phone.

With weariness in his voice, Vince said, "Chief sent every available unit to Crandon and called the Forest County Sherriff for backup. The three of us met late morning, and came up with a joint action plan. We put two mobile units at the trailhead, one tribal and one mine. The rest of the mobile units, both mine and the tribe's, are patrolling the streets. Everybody's patrolling solo, to free up enough bodies to stake out every pay phone in town. Meanwhile, the Sherriff has set up road blocks on every route out of town. All units have a recent photo of Flint, and a description of the clothing he wore when last seen. Everything was in place by mid-afternoon, well in advance of Flint's estimated time of arrival."

Rachel, impressed, "Huh … better than I expected, given the short notice."

Vince continued, "About 15 minutes ago, the trackers chasing Flint made Crandon. Unknown, is how much sooner Flint arrived. The main trail ends at a parking lot on a street at the edge of town. The guys in the mobile units never saw him. About a hundred yards short of the trail head, the dogs dragged the trackers off the main trail, and into the underbrush on an unbroken track parallel to the street. Apparently, Flint bushwhacked on this parallel track for about a quarter mile, and then came out of the woods, crossed the street, and disappeared. The dogs are spent, and had to be taken off the chase. No big loss, according to the trackers, they aren't worth a shit in town anyway. Bottom line, Flint's been at large in Crandon since some time before 5:45 PM. The trail was very hot, so it couldn't have been much before then."

Rachel sounded disappointed in him, "Unbelievable! That geezer is taking you all to school. Why the hell weren't the guys at the trail head lying in wait in the woods? After a 20-mile chase, did they really expect Flint to just waltz out into the parking lot, and wave hello?"

Too fatigued to put up a defense, Vince said, "It certainly does sound stupid. They're all big boys, and neither chief nor I thought we had to draw them a picture on what to do. In hindsight, apparently we were wrong."

Mind racing ahead, Rachel asked, "Okay, so what's next?"

Vince, energy waning, "We keep doing what we're

doing all night. The Sherriff's deputies keep up the road blocks. The chief's and my mobile units keep up the patrols. And we stay on every pay phone. If we don't have Flint by morning, he's either hiding somewhere in town, or been taken in by a friend. Tomorrow, we may have to mount a door-to-door search."

Rachel thought for a moment, "Let's talk again before starting any door-to-door search. All that visibility may do more harm than good. I'll sleep on it."

❋ ❋ ❋

After two sleep-disturbed nights, Rachel and Rose were beat. When Jake went down for the night, they decided to do the same. Though their interactions on the way to bed were tender and kind, neither had any interest in anything other than sleep. They didn't set an alarm, and mercifully, the phone never rang. Rachel woke naturally about 9:00 AM. By then, Rose was already attending to Jake, and seeing to coffee and breakfast. Rachel took a long hot shower, while pondering the wisdom of a door-to-door search. Afterward, she enjoyed a leisurely breakfast with Rose, and some quality time with Jake, before the phone rang again.

Rachel hustled to the study, answered on the fourth ring, and found Vince on the line. In a beaten down tone, he said, "Nothing turned up overnight. Then early this morning, the Sherriff's office received a breaking and entering call from the local rock quarry. Deputies investigated, and found the access gates breached on both ends of the quarry's private road. Chains on the gates were cut with a bolt-nippers, but nothing else was reported stolen or damaged. Here's the interesting part.

The private road runs mostly north and south, with one end within Crandon city limits, and the other dumping onto Hwy 55 south of the Sherriff's roadblock. Bottom line, Flint has a vehicle, he's got a big head start going south on Hwy 55, and could be anywhere by now."

Rachel laughed out loud. After taking a moment to compose herself, she said lightly, "I guess we won't need to search door-to-door."

Thankful for the break in tension, Vince quipped, "No, we won't. And if we ever catch that bastard, I'm going to hire him."

Rachel, playfully, "Great idea! In fact, maybe I'll make him your boss."

Vince groaned, "Ouch, I guess I deserved that." After a beat, he opined, "You seem in a better mood today."

Rachel admitted, "I am indeed. What wonders a good night's sleep can bring. Thanks for not calling in this latest mishap real time."

Vince sighed, "I didn't see the point. Flint had a big head start in a vehicle we couldn't ID. But a moment ago, another tidbit came in. That's why I called."

Curious, Rachel said, "I'm listening."

Vince said, "Once we knew Flint had a vehicle, the Sherriff, chief and I got together to regroup. A car rental place was mentioned, and that's the first I'd heard Crandon even had one. Here I am, sitting between them, unable to believe what I'm hearing. Crandon has a car rental, and neither of these dimwits, nor any of their officers, thought to check it."

Rachel burst into laughter again, and this time couldn't stop. All she could do was ride it out … tears streaming, sides aching, bent into a pretzel, and gasping for air. When the spasms subsided, Rachel croaked, "Oh my god! You, you can't make this shit up, can you? … a … a ha … a ha-ha." Then she lost it again.

Vince bided his time, and when Rachel resurfaced, said, "Chief dispatched a mobile unit, and word came back that Flint rented a car at 5:30 PM yesterday. He must've made Crandon earlier than the trackers thought. Anyway, they've got the make and model. Before putting out a state-wide bolo, chief wanted to talk it over with Long Body. He's on his way there now."

Rachel, after a beat, "I'd better call Long Body, and head that off. This whole fugitive arsonist thing won't hold up outside of Forest County. Vince, send your team home and go get some sleep. Let's talk tomorrow."

CHAPTER 7

Rachel's Bad Day – Monday; September 28, 1964; 7:00 AM

It'd been a week and a half since Rachel's minions let Flint slip away, and still no negative consequences. Cautiously optimistic, Rachel felt more upbeat with each passing day. Maybe Flint lost the goods in the fire. Maybe the close call made him think twice about delivering them. Maybe even with the goods in hand, the Evans's failed to raise enough money to pay off HMR. In two more days, she wouldn't give a shit what really happened, because the Evans farm would be hers.

Rachel continued to crack the whip over her team of lawyers and accountants. The suits were finally on track, and she believed they'd be ready for the state-agency meetings in Madison as early as the third week in October. Although itching to set those meetings up, she'd learned her lesson from prematurely seeking tribal council's approval. This time, she resolved to wait until HMR confirmed the Evans farm was hers.

As the Wolf family's sole survivor, Rachel was now the keeper of the family archives. In it, were written summaries of every successful Wolf family swindle going back to the beginning. Many times, over the years, she'd burned the midnight oil studying these "trophies". She was drawn to them. They enabled her to literally relive the thrills of her ancestors. More than that, they were a reliable source of physical pleasure. The physical response they aroused ... nape hairs standing, tingling, first in the breasts and groin, then everywhere, finally exploding seizure-like, into a full-body shiver ... was almost better than sex. Hell, it was better than sex. Reading the archives elevated her acuities, and enabled her to not only grasp the various strategies of her forebears, but envision variations that would've led to greater windfall profits than the original scams.

In Rachel's view, the current swindle was certainly her personal best, and perhaps the family's greatest of all time. It's the first to involve new legislation, and all the behind-the-scenes manipulation required to make that happen. In recent days, while waiting for the Evans farm death knell, she'd been drafting its summary while the details were still fresh in her mind. Writing the part about how she nabbed the Evans parcel without spending a dime, was particularly rewarding. She set an elegant trap, and a farmer's foolish pride and arrogance snapped it shut.

Lost in the joyful flow-state of her task, Rachel snapped out of her reverie at the knock on the study door. Rose peeked in, smiled, and silently mouthed *dinner time*. When Rachel joined them in the kitchen, Jake was busy making a mess in his high chair, while Rose was putting dinner on the table. She walked up behind her son to avoid his yucky hands, and planted a big kiss on top of his head. Then, she got him to squeal in delight at a funny face, before taking her seat.

Rose sensed Rachel's spirits were flying high. She knew her partner's manic highs brought with them soaring libido, and for fun, decided to froth that desire. Their gazes met, and Rose held hers a bit too long. Their feet touched under the table more often than random probability would suggest. By draping her long hair forward over the left shoulder, Rose exposed the long line of her neck on the right. Noticing Rachel's sideways glances, Rose enhanced the view by tilting her head, and used her left index finger to fiddle with a hank of hair. Caught looking, Rachel blushed, which evoked Rose's knowing smile ... the one that's not much more than a pout with a curl ... the one that drove Rachel wild. About then Rachel pointed a finger, "You stop that right now. God dammit, I'm wet already."

* * *

The following morning at 9:00 AM, Rachel and Rose were enjoying a leisurely breakfast and the sights and sounds of Jake munching Cheerios and jabbering to himself, when the doorbell rang. Rose hustled to the front door, then called for Rachel to come and sign for a delivery. These came all the time, and Rachel never gave it a second thought. After signing, she gave Rose a peck on the cheek, and continued on to the study with the envelope under her arm.

An hour later, Rachel reappeared in the kitchen noticeably pale, and asked not to be disturbed until dinner. When Rose offered to bring her something for lunch, Rachel distractedly waved it off, but suggested coffee and scones would be fine. Then, she pulled her son out of his chair for a hug, quickly passed him off to Rose, and hustled back to the study. Rose stood there, bouncing Jake on her hip, and watched as she went. She'd seen this before, something important business-wise had come up. In times like these, Rachel over-focused and any thought of a healthy lifestyle went right out the window. Rose prided herself in stepping in during these times and taking care of Rachel, whether she liked it or not.

After putting Jake down for his nap, Rose busied herself putting the finishing touches on a healthy lunch tray for Rachel. She smiled to herself, when the phone rang and was snatched mid-first-ring. Whatever was going on had Rachel on edge. She hummed contentedly, as the tray came together. She noticed an odd sound from the study, but thought nothing of it. Then later, she heard it again, and became more concerned. Finally, the tray was finished. In addition to coffee and scones, there were a variety of sliced cheeses and crackers, carrot and celery sticks with dip, blueberries, and fresh-sliced pineapple, strawberries, bananas, and apples. She grabbed the tray, and hurried to the study.

Rose didn't want to disturb Rachel. So, when she arrived, she set the tray on the hall table, and quietly slipped into the study to clear a place for it on the conference table. To Rose's surprise, rather than working at her desk, Rachel was standing in front of the fireplace, visibly agitated. Suddenly, Rachel grabbed a cut-glass tumbler off a nearby shelf, and hurled it into the fireplace.

Recognizing the sound as what she'd heard from the kitchen, Rose gasped, "My god Rachel, what're you doing? Those're Waterford crystal!"

Caught off guard, Rachel whirled, and her eyes narrowed as she struggled to process the intrusion. Red-faced and neck-veins popping, her eyes softened and fists relaxed as she recognized Rose. After regaining her composure, Rachel said, "I'm sorry Rose, I'm having a really bad day."

Stunned, having never seen this side of Rachel before, Rose just stood there, quivering and about to cry. Rachel stepped forward quickly and wrapped Rose in her arms, "There, there. Hey, everything's fine now, okay? I won't do it again, I promise." After Rose calmed and leaned in, Rachel asked, "Say, how're you doing with the coffee and scones?"

Rose stepped back and offered a tiny smile, "The tray is in the hall. I'm sorry, Rachel, I should've knocked before coming in. I needed to clear a place for the tray on the table, and didn't want to disturb you."

Rachel shook her head, "Shush now. You didn't do anything wrong."

* * *

After Rose brought in the tray and left, Rachel helped herself. While snacking, she castigated herself for losing her self-control. The last thing she needed right now, was for Rose to discover her true self. Keeping the various parts of her life separate, or compartmentalization as they say, had always been a strength. She needed to keep it that way.

After lunch, Rachel re-read the settlement package cover-to-cover. It wasn't any better the second time around. She picked up a pencil, and began sketching out her options on a pad of paper. While lost in this exercise, the phone rang again, and it was Vince, "Hello, Rachel. I'm just checking in."

Rachel, in a sarcastic tone, "Well, it's been an interesting day, Vince. For starters, a courier-package from Flint's insurance company came. I'd just finished skimming it when HMR called. Guess what? The Evans's paid off their loan. Using a cashier's check drawn on Oostburg Bank, no less. Bottom line, I need to pay for the fire or else, and oh by the way, my casino deal is dead, too."

Vince, after a beat, "Oostburg Bank. Why does that sound familiar?"

Rachel hissed, "I tried to buy them last year. Would've made them rich, but those hayseeds were too stupid to see it. Oh, and it gets better. HMR says the letter directs any communications to Ritter Law in Random Lake. Apparently, Ritter represents both the Evans family and the bank. Disputes between my family and lawyers named Ritter are noted all over the place, in my family archives. These little people just don't know when to quit. They'll be sorry."

Vince thought for a moment, then asked in a confused tone, "I get the payoff, but how'd the insurance company tie you to the fire?"

Rachel growled, "That's a really good question, Vince. How did they? As it turns out, they enclosed a really nice summary explaining exactly how. Let me read some to you … oh yes, here it is … here's an excerpt from the fire marshal's report … *a ground floor window on the backside of the house was breached, and accelerant and a flame tossed in … a circular cutout from the single-pane glass window was found lying on the ground nearby.*"

Vince exhaled like a popped balloon, "Oh shit. I told my guys to set the fire quietly, you know, so's not to wake Flint. They must've used a suction cup on the glass, run a circular glass cutter around it, and then tapped it free."

Rachel snapped, not bothering to hide her anger, "What the hell, Vince! Your goons left a circular cutout just lying there? I specifically told you to make it look like DIY wiring. If the fire had been declared accidental, the insurance company would've never looked into it. They'd have just paid the claim!"

Vince tried to dodge, "Well, not exactly. You never said make it look like DIY wiring. You said *looks like just another case of too much DIY wiring to me.* I took that to mean you planned to set something up with the fire marshal, you know, to get him to rule it your way."

Rachel hissed, "You took that to mean? Are you kidding me? I never said that! After more than a decade of doing my dirty work, you know damn well I say what I mean. If it isn't clear, ask for Christ's sake."

Vince, contrite, "Understood, Rachel. It won't happen again."

Undeterred, Rachel continued in a belittling tone, "And once the blaze is raging, what's the point of being quiet then? Why didn't your idiots at least try to make it less obvious. They could've smashed the cutout to smithereens, or taken it with them. But no, they just left it laying there? Even a bribed fire marshal never could've explained away a circular cutout just lying there."

Vince, wearing out his shoes, "I don't know, Rachel. I guess they just didn't think. I'll take them to the woodshed, and make sure it never happens again."

Once sure Vince understood the level of her displeasure, Rachel dialed back the drama and walked him through the rest of the insurance company's summary, including multiple eye witnesses of the Dodge 880s, four men with gas cans on the deer trail, positive ID that these same men had been at tribal council, and so on.

After hearing it all, Vince was still confused, "But none of that ties you to the fire."

Rachel, in a defeated tone, "Well, they've got DP setting the fire, and Long Body on tape identifying me as the owner of DP. Trust me, I've thought about throwing you under the bus, and claiming you acted alone. But thinking a few moves ahead, it wouldn't matter anyway. Flint must've delivered the goods, because the insurance company also provided a detailed blow-by-blow of the entire Evans farm saga. That fingers me, not you, with clear motive for the fire. Either I settle or fight it out in criminal and civil courts. If I fight, they'll take everything they know to the news media. Airing my dirty laundry in public could bring down my regional bank, and spoil any chance of developing a casino elsewhere."

Vince let that sink in, then said, "Jesus, what're you going to do?"

Rachel exhaled heavily, and said, "I'm still working on that. But unless I'm missing something, I've no choice but to settle. If it weren't for the insurance company, the rest of them wouldn't have deep enough pockets to go to war with me. Settling gets the big dog out of the picture. Later, I'll teach the rest of those assholes who they're dealing with."

Vince, bobbing and weaving to get back into Rachel's good graces, "Well, concerning payback, is there anything you want me to get started on now?"

Rachel thought about that, then said, "Yes, find Flint. When I tell Long Body the bad news, I'll ask him to help. Check in with him tomorrow. Also, start nosing around Sheboygan County. Find out who all does business with Oostburg Bank, and what James and Mary Evans are doing with their new lease on life."

Vince, in a relieved tone, "Roger that."

Before hanging up, Rachel added, "Oh, and Vince …
try not to screw it up."

* * *

Rachel spent the next several hours ruminating
over how to approach Long Body, and how much
information to share with him. When ready, she placed
the call, and Long Body said, "Hello, my friend. What can
I do for you today?"

Rachel, in a warm tone, "Dear friend, it's always
good to hear your voice. Unfortunately, I'm afraid I've got
some bad news. Remember that lapse in my judgement I
told you about? Well, it's bitten me in the rear end. The
Evans family paid off their loan, so for the time being
anyway, our casino project is on hold."

Long Body sounded disappointed in her, "I see. That
is very bad news." He thought a moment, then asked,
"Was it because of Flint?"

In a confident tone, Rachel said, "Yes, I believe it
was."

Long Body muttered, "Well, that figures. Little
Prairie band strikes again."

Rachel dropped her voice, "It gets better. Remember
that plausible deniability conversation we had, about the
fire?"

Cautious now, Long Body said, "Yes, I do. What of
it?"

Rachel, somewhat frostily, "Well, Flint's insurance
company has proposed a settlement, whereby I pay the
claim in exchange for them, Flint, the Evans', and the
Evans' lawyer and bank, all signing NDAs that'd bury the

dirty laundry."

Long Body thought about that, then said, "Huh, what're you going to do?"

Without hesitation, Rachel said, "I'm going to settle. Burying that dirty laundry means we're still free to develop a casino somewhere. Who knows, maybe even at HMR. Stranger things have happened."

Long Body's eye brows went up, "Maybe even at HMR? How's that even possible? Don't get me wrong, I'd love to continue there. But like you say, the loan's been paid off."

In a cold tone, Rachel said, "I can't answer that. It's another area where you'll want plausible deniability."

Message received, Long Body said, "I see. Well, is there anything I can do to help? You know, without getting into trouble."

Back to the warm tone, Rachel purred, "As a matter of fact, there is. We still want to find Flint. Any ideas on how you might help?"

Long Body thought about that, then said, "Hmm ... I'll have to think about that some more. But off the top of my head, I'd say I could enlist some trusted friends from outside the Little Prairie band to, you know, make subtle inquiries. Everybody knows about the fire, so asking about Flint's whereabouts shouldn't raise too many eye brows."

Delighted, Rachel said, "My man Vince will call you tomorrow."

CHAPTER 8

Pity Party Rachel-Style – Wednesday;
September 30, 1964; 5:00 AM

Rachel went all out to make the best use of her five business days. She totally focused on the settlement, by shedding all other concerns. Nightly sleep was dialed back to six hours, her lower limit to remain fully functional. When not sleeping, she remained cloistered in the study with the phone unplugged. She told Rose she was fighting off a serious business setback, and wasn't to be disturbed. For Jake, she and Rose came up with the ruse that mommy had to be gone for a few days. If Jake didn't know she was in the house, he wouldn't be a distraction.

Rose knew the drill, and seamlessly nannied Jake as if mommy was on travel, while at the same time catered to Rachel's every need, day and night. She knew exactly what Rachel needed to operate at full mental capacity. She brought breakfast, lunch, and dinner to the study on trays, and made sure the room was constantly stocked with fresh coffee, ice water, sliced fruit and berries on ice, and fresh croissants with butter and preserves. The nightly sex had gotten rougher and faster, a telltale sign that things weren't going well. But Rose held her tongue, and rode it out. Just to be safe, she hid all the remaining Waterford.

* * *

After working nonstop through three work days and the weekend, Rachel's energy began to fade. Having found no way out of her predicament didn't help. Grudgingly, she had to admire the airtight box she'd been lured into. She'd exhaustively explored every hypothetical option, and found nothing possible to accomplish in five business days more advantageous than simply settling. There wasn't any point in meeting with her adversaries, because she didn't have a credible alternative to pursue in negotiations. This particular battle had been lost, and she knew it.

Decision-made, Rachel moved on to the tedious process of following through with it. First thing Monday morning, she went to her bank to cut the check, sign the settlement, and have it notarized. Then she made copies, dropped the check and original in an envelope, and sent it on its merry way via courier. Afterward, at home in the study, she called her team of suits and told them to suspend preparations for the state-agency meetings. Instead, they should box the files, and have them sent by courier to her home. Next, she called Vince and Long Body, and filled them in. The HMR casino was a no-go, at least for now.

* * *

Mid-morning in a conversation with Rose, Rachel confided she'd been unable to prevent the business reversal, but at least the crisis was over. Her spirits were low, and she didn't bother to hide it. They talked some, or rather Rose tried to. But Rachel bobbed and weaved, and soon Rose relented. Rachel knew her partner was only trying to make her feel better, but didn't want to get into the details with her. Their conversation turned to Jake, who was currently napping. Conspiratorially, they bantered over how to reveal to Jake that mommy was home, and how excited they knew he'd be.

Over the next several days, Rachel did her best to keep up appearances with Jake and Rose, but her heart wasn't in it. Sure, she'd had minor setbacks before. But for the first time in her life, she hadn't gotten something that she really-really wanted. She was accustomed to being dominant and imposing her will. Being told what to do, and doing it, didn't sit well. As she went through the motions of caring for Jake ... toilet training, feeding and playing with him ... she struggled to stay present. In the back of her mind, she was second-guessing decisions and totting up her financial losses. Almost as bad, her tender moments with Rose felt more like out-of-body experiences with her as a spectator. She'd entice and tantalize to get what she wanted physically, but in spirit she wasn't really there.

Feeling vulnerable and uncertain, persistently over a period of time, was new to Rachel. In the past, she'd always been able to disavow such feelings, or at least easily overcome them. But this time was different. Her financial losses had been staggering. She couldn't stop the gears in the back of her head from dwelling on each loss one-by-one, over and over. All of those pro bono hours spent on the committee, looking into the conflict between the tribes and the state's sportsmen. Then, the untold hours to herd the committee to recommend gaming, politick for the law, build tribal relationships, and so on. Spending time was bad enough, but hemorrhaging money was even worse ... for land, attorneys, accountants, marketeers, security, and whatnot.

As grievous as these losses were, Rachel could barely contain her rage at being forced to pay the settlement costs. The fire costs were an insult, but being forced to pay the investigative costs to prove she owed them ... now that was a total outrage. Then, on the same day, to lose the Evans farm. Nabbing that farm for free was intended to offset most of the other costs, but now it's gone too. She'd spent her entire life serving up indignities like these to other people, but not once had she ever been on the receiving end. That is, until now.

✻ ✻ ✻

After enduring a week of Rachel clearly off her game, Rose finally worked up the courage to intervene. With Jake down for the night, she brought a wine bottle and glasses to the family room. There, she found Rachel staring, trance-like, into the flames in the fireplace. Rose waited at the threshold until Rachel became aware of her presence.

Rachel smiled weakly, "Thanks, I could use a glass of wine."

Rose poured them each a glass, and said softly, "Rachel, can we talk?"

Rachel looked at her, evaluating, "That depends on

the topic."

Rose settled into the comfy leather chair next to Rachel's, crossed her legs, and said in a concerned tone, "I know enough not to ask about your business. But you haven't been yourself since the setback, and I'm worried about you. What happened to that strong, confident woman I used to know? You know, the invincible conqueror that used to strut all over the face of the earth." Then, after a pause and a full-on blush, she teased, "And where's that insatiable woman with the audacity to suggest unthinkably naughty things to do in the bedroom?"

Rachel looked at her, reevaluating, "You're blushing. Did something cross your mind that I can help you with?"

Flustered, Rose shook her head, "Don't you dare change the subject. It's been a week, and from all appearances, you're still in a downward spiral. Even Jake has noticed. He told me *'Mommy sad'* when I put him to bed tonight."

Rachel winced, "Oh my god, did he really? I'd no idea."

Rose nodded, "Yes, he did. Look, you've never been this bad before. I remember you once being, oh I don't know, maybe half this bad. That time you went to Wolf's Run for a few days, and came back as good as new."

Rachel jerked upright and her eyes widened, "Wolf's Run!" She bounced her palm off her forehead, "Why didn't I think of that?"

❊ ❊ ❊

The next day Rachel left for Wolf's Run, a 1,280-acre estate on the Menominee River, which she inherited from her late parents. The Menominee flows into Green Bay, and defines much of the border between Wisconsin and Upper Michigan. The estate was on the Wisconsin-side, not far from Iron Mountain. According to family legend, the Wolfs acquired the land shortly after Wisconsin became a state in 1848, and selected the specific parcel for its multiple easy river crossings into Upper Michigan. You know, in case a speedy escape from the law was required.

The family grew to enjoy hiking in the pastoral solitude of the heavily wooded wilderness. Common sights included bear, deer, otter, badger, wolf, coyote, rabbit, squirrel, eagle, hawk, ruffed grouse, and a host of songbirds. During spring, summer and fall, the river, tributaries, and nearby lakes provided some of the best muskie, walleye, and smallmouth bass fishing in the country. In the fall, there's also hunting. In winter, ice fishing, snow shoeing, and cross-country skiing could be enjoyed on the property, and downhill skiing was only a quick trip away.

Rachel's parents had always left Wolf's Run vacant between visits, and as a consequence, much of their time there was spent on bucolic maintenance tasks, which they seemed to enjoy. Rachel preferred her visits to be strictly R&R, and employed a live-in couple to keep up the house and grounds, and cook, clean and do laundry when she visited. Craving solitude, Rachel decided to drive north herself, in her black Ford T-Bird Landau. She called ahead so dinner would be waiting and the hearth glowing, upon arrival. On the way north she enjoyed the scenery, with its many shades of brown interspersed with evergreens, so typical of November in this part of Wisconsin.

Wolf's Run was Rachel's favorite place on earth. She

carried with her always, the imprints of life-changing events she'd experienced there. For Rachel, in a sense, the place held magical restorative powers. Upon arrival, she marched up the path to what the family historically referred to as the cabin. Nowadays, calling this dwelling a cabin was a bit of a misnomer, to say the least. Although tiny and rustic in the 1840s, today's large country-gentry main house and outbuildings looked more like the setting for an Eddie Bauer photo shoot.

Rachel greeted the caretaking couple, asked the husband to fetch the bags, and the wife to have dinner served in an hour. Then she made herself a Maker's Mark Manhattan garnished with orange zest and a bourbon cherry, and enjoyed it by the fire. Afterward, she went to her room for a quick shower and change. Dinner consisted of a ribeye, medium-rare, baked potato with all the fixings, and crisp-tender roasted fresh broccolis covered with garlic, lemon, and parmesan cheese. It all went down nicely with a full-bodied California red zinfandel wine. After dinner, Rachel donned her coat and went for a leisurely stroll. Upon returning, she arranged for an early breakfast, and retired for the evening.

For recentering and rejuvenating herself at Wolf's Run, Rachel had a tried-and-true routine. She'd get an early start, pick one of her favorite life-changing experiences, warm up mentally by hiking her favorite trails while pulling up the memories, and then relive the event by retracing the steps where it actually occurred. As she lay in bed, Rachel considered which of her personal-best moments to reenact over the next few days. She knew she'd hit a new low, and reliving any one experience might not be enough to bring her all the way back. She smiled inwardly as a plan began to coalesce. She decided to relive what she considered to be her two biggest Wolf's Run life-changers, one-per-day, in chronological order. If that didn't put her at the top of her game, nothing would.

CHAPTER 9

The Evans's Dilemma – Tuesday; October
17, 1964; 12:00 Noon

T he annual Sheboygan County Fair was something the Evans family always looked forward to. Held at the Plymouth fairgrounds on Labor Day weekend and the half-week before, the kids enjoyed rides and games on midway, while Overdrive and Mary gabbed with friends in the show barns, or at the farm implement dealer displays. This year's fair plans exploded at the end of August, when HMR dropped their pay-in-full bombshell. Overdrive and Mary skipped the fair altogether, but had Jumbo shuttle his siblings there a few times, to keep up morale and a façade of normalcy.

As Bob Dylan would say *the times, they are a changing.* In the fall of 1964, word of the NFO was spreading like wildfire in the Wisconsin dairy farming community. A fledgling Sheboygan County chapter had formed, and for the first time there'd been an NFO booth at the county fair. Overdrive and Mary missed seeing it, of course, but they'd already decided to look into the NFO. Having a local chapter made the search for information that much easier.

In late October after the fall harvest was done, Overdrive and Mary invited a local NFO-member farmer and his wife to lunch at the Evans farm. The Evans' were acquainted with these people, admired them as successful farmers, and wanted to learn more about the NFO. Over lunch, the Evans' were treated to a vivid description of a peer farm family's journey on its way to joining the NFO. There'd been no sales pitch to join. Instead, they just told their personal story and left behind some NFO print material. They said feel free to call with any questions. Then in jest, they said if the Evans' had a better idea on how to save family farming in America's Dairyland, they'd damn well better call about that, too.

Overdrive and Mary devoured the NFO information separately, and decided to head to Harbor Lights after the evening milking for privacy, while discussing whether or not to join. Once at the rustic resort, they exchanged pleasantries with the regulars at the bar, grabbed a few beers, and took seats at their favorite table in a quiet corner. Bursting with enthusiasm, Overdrive said, "Did you read '*Who speaks for the farmer*'? That really resonated with me. It's the talk the NFO president gave last April at UW River Falls. What's his name again?"

Mary bobbed her head, "Oren Lee Staley. That really did hit the nail on the head. Nobody speaks for the farmer, and that's why we need the NFO."

Animated, arms waving, Overdrive said, "Sounds like the NFO is really taking off. Did you see the write up on their national convention? Held in Minneapolis, just last month. They had a huge crowd."

Mary, bouncing with excitement, "Sure did, wish we could've been there. Collective bargaining makes a lot of sense. The milk processors don't care about us. They set the price of raw milk to maintain a minimum profit margin, and gouge when they can. If the market turns down, they pass it along to us. If it turns up, we never see it and they pocket the difference."

Overdrive nodded, "That's exactly right. Plus, there's only one processor collecting milk in our area. It's a monopoly and we've nowhere else to go. But if the NFO can aggregate us, maybe they can make something happen."

Mary dropped her voice, "Can you imagine how good it'd feel to find another processor, and tell this one to stick it? Good lord, after all those years of *'here's what you get, take it or leave it.'* The NFO even brings in their own bulk milk trucks to haul, if necessary."

Overdrive, head bobbing, "Yeah, I remember reading that. They said haulers are almost always in cahoots with the lone processor, getting kickbacks. In return, they price gouge the cost to haul anywhere else, so we can't afford to switch. And all these years, we've been giving that driver a quart of brandy for Christmas."

Mary looked at him, "It's all pretty disappointing, isn't it? I mean, none of them seem to care if we can make a decent living, no matter how hard we and our kids work. If it weren't for folks like us, they'd have nothing to haul or process."

Overdrive darkened, "Well, according to them it's our fault, because we haven't gotten big enough yet. Economies of scale, they say. Of course, pretty soon you're so big a family can't handle it anymore, and you end up with agribusiness. I've been reading about those giant dairy operations in California. Huge herds on hardly any land, so they truck in the feed. Not enough land for spreading shit, so they build giant man-made lakes to hold it. Lagoons, they call them. They burst now and then, or overflow in a heavy rain. When that happens, it pollutes the groundwater forever. When one local authority shuts them down, they just pick up and move to a different jurisdiction. Processors and haulers could care less, so long as the supply of cheap milk keeps coming."

Disheartened, Mary muttered, "People around here enjoy their country drives, pretty red barns and green pastures dotted with Holsteins. But do they even know it's because of folks like us? Once we're gone, it'll be lagoons, stench, flies, water unsafe to drink, and feedlots full of shit-caked, mistreated animals."

Overdrive looked at her, reevaluating, "More often than not, people go with the flow. It's only human nature, plus they've got their own worries. Family farmers in dairying have a problem, and we need to fix this ourselves."

Mary, in a resigned tone, "You're right, we need to fix this. So, what about the NFO? Did you notice we'd need to sign an agreement that names the NFO as our bargaining agent if we joined? How do you feel about that?"

Overdrive sat back and exhaled heavily, "Well, it's certainly something new. We've never had an agent before. But it makes sense in a way. How else could they aggregate a bunch of farmers together, and negotiate on our behalf? Even so, I'd feel more comfortable if we talked to Dad before signing up."

Mary nodded, "Let's have him over for lunch tomorrow."

* * *

Over lunch the next day, Overdrive and Mary filled Old Bill in on what they'd learned about the NFO, and asked his advice on whether to join. Old Bill leaned back in his chair, looked from one to the other, and said, "Boy, I don't know. Things like that can get pretty dicey in a hurry. You might've missed it in the wake of HMR's big surprise, but two farmers died during an NFO holding action in early September. It was over in central Wisconsin."

Mary gasped, "W-what!"

Overdrive, in a skeptical tone, "Are you sure? I never heard about that."

Old Bill nodded, "Yes, I'm sure. The NFO was trying to hold cattle off the market with a demonstration at a stockyard. A cattle truck driver got mad, and drove right into the crowd of picketers, killing two."

Mary did the sign of the cross, "Good lord."

Old Bill held up a heavy index finger, "There's more. I heard most of the farmers supplying milk to Lake-to-Lake signed up to have NFO be their agent. The coop refused to negotiate, so the NFO is planning a protest at the coop's annual meeting in Luxemburg, up near Green Bay. That might get ugly, too."

Overdrive shook his head, "Huh, hadn't heard about that either."

Old Bill shrugged, "There's no shame in that, son. You two have been pretty busy with HMR." Then he mimed a shudder, "The whole idea just takes me back to the Great Depression. There'd been milk strikes back then too, you know."

Wide-eyed, Overdrive said, "There were?"

With a far-off look, Old Bill said, "Yes, and they didn't end well either. Milk prices had dropped so low in 1933, dairy farmers were going broke left and right. There'd been multiple strikes that year. Farmers tried to hold milk off the market until they got a reasonable price. They set up pickets around creameries to block haulers. In response, the creameries had their haulers form convoys, and hired armed guards to protect them. Lots of milk was dumped, or tainted with kerosene. Pitched battles broke out all over the state. Seven creameries were bombed, including ones near Plymouth, Fond du Lac, and Belgium. The governor sent in the national guard to put it down."

Mary gasped again, "Are you sure?"

Overdrive's eyebrows went up, "I was a teen by then, why don't I remember any of this?"

Old Bill eyed his son, "Probably because you weren't much interested in newspapers back then, and I kept us out of it."

Overdrive scoffed, "You stood on the sidelines? How could you? You just stood by and watched your friends and neighbors go under?"

Old Bill pointed a finger at his son, and said sternly, "Listen up, dumbass, it wasn't that simple. Things were even more corrupt then, than they are now. The processors had the governor in their hip pocket. People in all walks of life were hurting, not just us. I looked into getting involved, but decided another path provided a better chance to survive. The fact that I still had a farm when you wanted to take one over, proves I made the right decision."

Mary intervened, and tried to lighten things up, "Look Dad, your big lug of a son, also known as my husband, meant no disrespect, okay? But you've really sparked my curiosity. What'd you do?"

Old Bill, through a Cheshire cat grin, "I gambled at

cards down in Cascade. Cheated actually, with the help of the ancestors. Doesn't that husband of yours tell you anything? I won enough to make upgrades and pass inspection for Grade A. At the time, farmers got paid almost double for beverage milk, compared to milk for cheese and butter. You know, speaking of ancestors, you might want to find out what they think before going off half-cocked, and joining the NFO."

* * *

Overdrive and Mary took Old Bill's advice, and went to his shack after the evening milking. Old Bill had everything ready, and after the bridge was opened, he began chattering away in Welsh. He brought the ancestors up to speed on the NFO, why joining was under consideration, and asked what their advice might be.

The room exploded with spirit voices speaking the alien tongue. Old Bill struggled to keep up with the conversation, and on several occasions had to interrupt to slow it down. Frustrated, Old Bill said, "We've apparently struck a multi-generational nerve. They're arguing among themselves. Truth be told, they're rudely talking over each other and I can't make a lot of it out."

Overdrive's eyebrows shot up, "Jesus! That's never happened before. What's it all about?"

Mary, eyes like saucers, "My ears are burning, and I can't even understand the language."

As it continued at a fevered pitch, Old Bill shook his head, and said, "Goddammit, they've got all day to chew each other's asses. I'll see if I can get them to show some respect to the living, and boil all that vitriol into useful advice."

Old Bill waded back into the shouting match, and did his best to impose some rules of decorum. Nothing changed, and for the first time in Overdrive's memory, Old Bill lit into his ancestors with anger rather than deference. After repeated verbal assaults, the chatter gradually began to evolve, and eventually de-escalated to some semblance of previous bridges.

Weary, Old Bill said, "There's not much they can all agree on, other than the NFO sounds like the latest in a long line that includes the Grange, National Farmers Union, Farmers Alliance, United Farmers League, and so on. To hear them tell it, all these groups had noble goals but never accomplished a thing. The problem is, farmers can't be unified, even in pursuit of their own self-interest. There're always a few delusional ones that won't participate, and ruin it for the rest. You know the type ... they fancy themselves as the last bastions of rugged individualism. Their own ideology makes them easy to manipulate. Whenever the folks ripping off farmers need to break a strike or a picket line, they claim the instigators are commie-led, and the delusional farmers break ranks."

Overdrive muttered, "Well, shit. That sounds pretty defeatist to me. What're they saying, don't bother trying?"

Mary said pointedly, yet in a respectful way, "I agree. We came here for advice. Don't they have any?"

Old Bill nodded his understanding, and began to chatter in Welsh again. The ensuing babble was lively but more respectful, and Old Bill caught Mary's eye and winked. Head bobbing, he occasionally interjected a sentence or two to steer the discussion, but in general let it play out on its own. When the rumble died down, Old Bill said, "They can't agree on overarching advice per se, but each generation that farmed in Wisconsin has opinions to share. Interested in a history lesson?"

Overdrive and Mary looked at each other, shrugged, and said "Sure."

Old Bill passed that along, and the ancestors chattered back. After a moment, he cleared his throat, and said, "I'll do my best to give you crisp summaries of the key viewpoints. In the earliest days of Wisconsin dairying, the ancestors produced milk and made butter for family use. But production soon exceeded need, and milk and butter didn't keep, so they made cheese, which could be stored in a spring house or root cellar. What wasn't eaten, they bartered to village storekeepers for household necessities, or to peddlers that came around, for wares they carried. They made the circuit to nearby villages to get the best deal."

Overdrive caught his father's eye, "Well, we don't really barter with storekeepers and peddlers anymore, but I think I get the point. Don't blindly trust whoever's buying your product to give you a fair deal."

Mary chimed in, "Huh … in other words, having options is a good thing."

Old Bill nodded, "That's my take on it. Now, as the years went on, local cheese factories started popping up, and the ancestors started selling milk to them. Generally, there'd be a self-employed cheesemaker with investors, or patrons. Usually, the patrons held title to the cheese, set the cheesemaker's compensation, sourced the milk, determined the style of cheese to make and who to sell it to, handled the sale, and hauled the product. Patrons, with their fast-talk and slick-dress, couldn't be trusted. Whenever the price of milk dropped too low, a frequent occurrence, the ancestors reverted to home cheesemaking and competitive barter."

Overdrive's eyebrows went up, "Huh. Essentially the same message."

Mary added, "I'm beginning to see a pattern here."

Old Bill bobbed his head, "Okay now, a little later, milk had to be sold no matter what. That's because home cheesemaking became unviable, due to the expense of new sanitation regulations. But by then, cheese factories were everywhere, so for a time it'd been possible to compete factories against each other to ensure a fair milk price. But before long, professional cheese buyers were coming around and swindling the cheesemakers, who then slashed what they'd pay for milk to stay afloat. Both now being screwed by middlemen, farmers and cheesemakers joined forces to form dairy boards of trade. For a time, these provided transparent forums for auctioning off cheese to the highest bidder. But soon scoundrels figured a way to circumvent the boards, too, and milk prices swung wildly. To survive, the ancestors diversified by husbanding a variety of animals for meat, and by growing cash crops."

Overdrive shook his head, "Good grief, running the farm and all, how'd they ever have time to keep up with all the shenanigans going on around them?"

Hand to head, Mary said, "All this's making my head spin."

Old Bill shrugged, "I hear you, good old days my ass. Anyway, price-fixing and whatnot went largely unchecked, so the dairy boards failed. After that, several farmer-led actions tried to pick up the pieces. The first leveraged Wisconsin's first legislation authorizing cooperatives, which passed in 1911. After organizing meetings at the Plymouth fairgrounds in 1912 and 1913, the *Sheboygan County Cheese Producers Federation* began operations in 1914. For the first time, farmers stored and marketed cheese themselves, rather than through dealers. The second, was the establishment in 1921, of the *Farmers' Call Board* in Plymouth. These both failed when the Great Depression hit, which led to the 1933 milk strikes."

Overdrive, elbows on knees and head in hands, "Jesus! If I'd known all this, I never would've gone dairy farming."

Mary scoffed, "Oh, who're you trying to kid. You fell out of the womb looking for a cow to milk, and you know it."

Eyes a twinkling, Old Bill said, "Now children, behave."

CHAPTER 10

Decision Time Nears – Wednesday;
November 4, 1964; 8:00 PM

I t's the first week of November, and harvest season was finally winding down. To occupy his mind during evening milking, Overdrive reviewed where things stood. He'd hired a nearby farmer to bring his own equipment and pick the ear corn. The crib was already full, and the rest of the crop would be picked over the next few days, and stored at the coop. The silos were full, but a few acres of leftover field corn remained. They'd been chopping it daily into bunk wagons as fodder for the herd, and at the rate they're going, it'll give out in four days. That's when they'll cull the herd, and hire a cattle trucker to haul the unlucky ones to the Milwaukee stockyards. Once right-sized, the herd will spend the rest of the winter pampered in the barn, each cow in its own stanchion. None too soon, since the weather was getting nastier by the day.

Overdrive had already planned his land use and crop rotations for next year. He and Mary decided to drop some of the rental land and forego cash crops to give the family a breather. With Old Bill a year older and Jumbo's plans after graduation uncertain, they couldn't risk attempting a redo of last year. Overdrive had already plowed the poor-yielding alfalfa lands he planned to reseed to corn next year, and he'd made good progress on the lands that'll remain in corn. Like last year, he and Jumbo had been sharing nighttime frost plowing duties. In another few weeks, the plowing should be done.

Also in progress, was the annual race to clean the manure out of the heifer barns before it froze solid. This year, old man winter would be beaten handily. Overdrive smiled to himself, as he thought about his second son, Joe. What a difference a year makes ... Joe had mastered the scoop tractor. It takes a certain feel for the hydraulics and side brakes, to undulate the bucket's blade-edge up-and-down and waggle it side-to-side while ramming forward into the packed manure. At the same time, it's important to establish a rocking motion, through rhythmic clutching and shifting, to repeatedly ram the manure and break it free. Joe had it down pat, and at the current rate, all three heifer barns should be cleaned in another week. Sure, Joe still whined incessantly and had a smart mouth, but Overdrive was genuinely proud of him.

The thought of what Mary, Kathy and Marie had accomplished this year also made Overdrive's heart swell with pride. They'd crammed the cellar floor-to-ceiling with garden and orchard bounty. He'd never before seen it so full. Rack upon rack, shelf upon shelf. Jars, crocks and bushel baskets were everywhere.

While these thoughts occupied Overdrive on the surface, the NFO decision continued to inhabit the back of his mind. Over the past few weeks, he'd reread the NFO literature, and replayed in his mind the ancestral advice, over and over again. He'd even called his cattle trader friend, Gib Buyer, to see what he thought. He'd looked at it from every angle. Early on, which way he leaned, varied by day. But for three days straight, he'd come down on the same side. Overdrive now knew what he wanted to do, but needed to learn where Mary stood. That evening after milking, they agreed to head to Harbor Lights to make a joint decision.

After the evening's work was done, by coincidence, Overdrive and his four boys all converged on the house at the same time. While crowded into the mud room changing out of their barn clothes, Overdrive noticed bloody wounds all over David's arms and torso, and asked, "What the hell happened to you?"

David examined himself, "Nothing. Just playing a game with John."

Overdrive rotated his steely gaze to John, "What game?"

John looked down, and said weakly, "Jim Taylor up the middle."

Confused, Overdrive asked, "Jim who?"

Trying to be helpful, Jumbo chimed in, "Jim Taylor, dad. You know, the fullback of the Green Bay Packers. Number 31. Lombardi claims he's the toughest back in the NFL. Every time he breaks into the open, he looks for a defender to hit. Runs right at him, and rams him head-on. Sacrifices yards that way, but wears a defense down over four quarters."

Overdrive chuckled, "Sounds more stupid than tough. I'm no expert on football, but I thought the idea was to get into the end zone."

Joe added his two cents, "That is stupid. Even I know that."

Hyped, John interrupted, "Yeah, but did you see him last Sunday? On this one play, he left a trail of broken bodies all the way to the end zone. One of those guys had to be carried off the field!"

After a joyful shudder, Jumbo gushed, "That was a thing of beauty!"

Overdrive had suspicions that John and Jumbo were feeding him a line of bullshit, but he wasn't certain. He looked from one to the other, then said, "So, tell me about this game. Jim Taylor up the middle."

After some nods and eye contact, John did the talking, "Well, we play it up in the haymow ... only after chores are done, of course. You start at the edge of the hay stack, and lay two rows of bales on the empty barn floor, end-to-end, leading away from the hay. Four to six bales, end-to-end, works best. You space the two rows just far enough apart to run between. Then you pile a second tier of bales on top of both rows, but these are askew so the running lane is blocked alternately, from the left and the right. Then you add a third tier, straight and end-to-end like the first. When done, you back up to the far wall and run like hell into the blocked lane. If you make it all the way to the hay stack, it's a touchdown."

With a skeptical frown, Overdrive thought about that a moment, then said, "Let me get this straight. You go to all that trouble to set up bales, and then you just run into them, and cut yourself up on hay stubble. Does that about cover it?"

John nodded, "Yup."

Overdrive shook his head, "That's about the stupidest game I've ever heard of. Who made that up?"

John met his father's eye, "I did, sir." Then he looked over at his bloodied brother, "But the cuts usually aren't so bad. I might've forgotten to tell David the part about wearing a long-sleeved denim shirt or jacket."

Overdrive muttered, "Jesus, and I thought you were the smart one. David, put your shirt back on before your mother sees you. This all stays between us."

As Overdrive stood to leave, Joe whined, "Oh, come on Dad. John deserves a whipping, doesn't he? I mean, if it'd been me ..."

* * *

Overdrive and Mary were pleasantly surprised to find their good friends, Scully and Jan, at the bar when they walked into Harbor Lights. Overdrive wisecracked, "Good grief, nowadays I guess they'll let anybody in here. This place used to have standards."

Scully shot back, "Well, according to the barkeep, you two have been regulars here for years, so any past standards couldn't have been very high."

Mary laughed, "Guilty, as charged." Then, to Jan, "I thought your go-to place was Weyers's, on the other side of the lake. It's closer to home, isn't it?"

Jan smiled, and said, "We like the Friday night fish fry over there, but in general, any place with a bar is fair game for us. That's why we live in Cascade, you know, plenty of options."

Mary and Jan hugged, and moved to the other end of the bar to get caught up. Overdrive ordered a round of beers for everyone, then leaned toward his friend, "Scully, what do you know?"

Scully, eyebrows up, "I was about to ask you the same thing. How's your father doing?"

Confused, Overdrive asked, "What do you mean?"

Scully eyed his friend for a moment, "You haven't heard, have you?"

Overdrive, a trifle impatiently, "Heard what?"

Scully leaned in, "Well, there was an accident on Art's corner today, and the wrecks slid into his shop and caused a fire."

Overdrive's lower jaw dropped, "You mean Dad didn't stop, and somebody plowed into him?"

Scully turned in his stool, "No-no, well that's what happened, but it wasn't Old Bill that pulled out and got hit. Anyway, the wrecks barely missed Art in the service bay. With some quick thinking, he got the drivers to safety, but with all the commotion, he forgot about Old Bill sitting in his office, reading the newspaper."

Overdrive's eyes popped, "W-what?"

Scully, talking fast, "The whole place was engulfed in flames and the fire trucks had arrived before Art remembered. The volunteer fire fighters were about to go in after him, when Old Bill kicked his way through the glass door and stumbled outside in a billow of smoke."

Overdrive stared at Scully in disbelief, looking for the telltale shit-eating grin. When one never came, he muttered, "You'd better not be pulling my leg, Scully. Not on something like this. It wouldn't be funny."

Scully held up three fingers in a Boy Scout salute, "It's the god's honest truth, I swear."

Concerned now, Overdrive asked, "Is he okay? Dad, I mean."

Scully's eyes narrowed, "As far as I know. To hear Art tell it, Old Bill kicked the door into a million pieces and stomped his way through the billowing smoke, cussing up a blue streak. When the smoke cleared, Old Bill looked himself over, and noticed a shard of glass sticking out of his shoulder. Then, he muttered *sonofabitch* and grabbed it, yanked it out, and flung it away. The fire guys stopped the bleeding, and somebody ran him to Plymouth for stitches. Your Dad's a tough old bird, he'll be alright." He paused for emphasis, then said, "How he ever sired a wuss like you, is beyond me."

Overdrive laughed, "Ha, so now I'm the wuss. Then, how come when we joined the Army, they gave me a Sherman tank, and you a rifle?"

Scully beamed, "Well, unlike you, they noticed I came self-equipped with a giant gun." They went on like that for a while, then Overdrive caught Mary's eye, and they excused themselves and took seats at their favorite table.

Overdrive whispered to Mary, "Did Jan tell you about Dad?"

Mary's eyes narrowed, "Yes. Oh my god, James. He could've been killed!" They talked a bit more about the accident, then moved on to why they'd come.

Overdrive dropped his voice, "Mary, what're your thoughts on joining the NFO? The Sheboygan County chapter meets next week. If we're joining, we should be there."

Mary looked down at her beer for a moment, "What stuck with me most, from the ancestors, was the fact that they always fought to maintain enough negotiating leverage on their markets to survive. We haven't been doing that, at least up to now. I think we've got to do something."

Overdrive took a moment to organize his thoughts, then said, "I agree, we've got to do something. And I think the NFO is the only game in town. The Farm Bureau folks are really nice. I like them, I really do. But when you talk to them, they seem fine with taking whatever price for milk is offered. When things are tight, they blame themselves for not investing more during the good times, and getting bigger. It hasn't dawned on them that beyond a certain size, a family can't keep up anymore, and the margins aren't big enough to hire help."

Mary held up her bottle, "To the NFO, then."

Overdrive clinked his with hers, and said, "Maybe we should run this by Dad again before, you know, actually joining."

Mary nodded, "I agree, let's talk to him tomorrow." Then, with an impish grin, "Sounded like John Wayne, the way he escaped the fire. I can't wait to hear Old Bill's story!"

❋ ❋ ❋

The next morning, Old Bill called to say he's under the weather, and unable to help with cleaning the heifer barns. Mary smiled at the little white lie, covered the receiver and whispered, "It's your father saying he's under the weather, and not coming out to the farm. How about I tell him we'll be there at noon with a picnic lunch, to cheer him up."

Overdrive flashed thumbs up, "Never known him to turn down a free meal."

Mary winked, got back on the line, and wouldn't take no for an answer. Afterward, she said, "He really didn't want to see us today. No mention of the accident, either. Maybe he's hurt worse than we think."

Overdrive thought about that, "I don't think so. He just hates people fussing over him, and he's probably embarrassed over not being up for a day's work."

Too smeary for field work, Overdrive spent the morning greasing the plow and changing its blades. Mary got caught up with housework, and prepared the picnic basket. During the ride to Cascade, they decided to lead with the NFO discussion over lunch, and leave the accident to last. When they knocked, Old Bill hollered for them to come in, but remained seated in his stuffed chair.

After exchanging pleasantries, Mary sized up the situation, and said, "Dad, stay where you are. We'll have our picnic right there." While she set her basket on the foot stool and positioned everything within reach, Overdrive fetched a third chair from the kitchen.

Once settled, everybody dug in. There were summer sausage and sharp cheddar cheese sandwiches, apple slices, potato salad, and beers to drink. Old Bill started to move his left arm to grab a sandwich, winced, pulled it back, and reached across himself with his right. Then he said, "To what do I owe this great honor?"

Overdrive said, "Dad, we need to talk some more about whether or not to join the NFO. Since the bridge, we've been processing the advice, and both came down on the side of joining. What do you think? And don't hold back."

Old Bill swallowed a bite of sandwich, then said, "First, why don't you talk me through how you came to that decision."

Overdrive munched an apple slice, and said, "Fair enough. In a nutshell, every generation worked hard to retain some sort of leverage to get a fair deal for what they produced. They didn't just passively accept what was offered."

Mary added, "Up until now, we'd always thought our job was to produce milk, period. We never gave leverage, or negotiating, much thought. Now we realize we should've."

Old Bill winced again, then said, "Those are fair points. You know, I probably deserve some of the blame for you two not realizing this sooner. After the switch to Grade A, things were pretty good on the farm. By the time you took over, even I hadn't worried about anything but producing milk for years. I should've done a better job communicating that it hadn't always been that way."

After a sip of beer, Overdrive said, "Look Dad, we didn't come here looking for you to take the blame for our problems."

Old Bill nodded, "I know son, but a father can't help but feel guilt when he realizes he could've done better. Taking the long view, leverage is essential if you're overly dependent on one product. Another strategy that can work, is to stay diversified. Then, when milk prices go south, you can rotate to other products."

Mary's eyebrows went up, "What do you mean?"

Old Bill pondered that as he put down his sandwich, and forked in a mouthful of potato salad from the plate on his lap. After swallowing, he said, "Well, over the years that farm has produced beef, veal, pork, feeder pigs, lamb, mutton, wool, chicken, timber, fire wood, peas, sweet corn, and probably other things I can't remember right now."

Overdrive shook his head, "Dad, I think we're way past being able to rely on diversity. Dairying is capital-intensive, and we just made a big investment to double our milk production. With our current assets and manpower, if milk went south, those sidelines would never be able to make up the difference."

Old Bill put down his fork, and awkwardly reached

across his body to snag another apple slice from the bowl on the foot stool. Then, he said, "So, you think the only realistic course of action is to get some negotiating leverage on milk."

Overdrive nodded, "Yes."

Mary said, "I agree."

Old Bill narrowed his eyes, and looked from one to the other, "And you think the NFO is your best bet."

Overdrive bobbed his head, "Yes."

Mary sat upright, "Absolutely."

Old Bill said wisely, "Well, there's your answer. Join the NFO."

The room grew silent as they all pondered the consequences of that. When lunch was finished, Mary packed away the dishes and napkins, and Overdrive said, "So Dad, what happened at Art's yesterday?"

Old Bill winced, "God dammit, that Art never could keep his mouth shut!"

CHAPTER 11

Overdrive's Lapse in Judgment – Saturday;
December 5, 1964; 2:00 PM

The glorious day ... blue skies, windless, nearly 60 F ... was totally out of character for the first Saturday in December. Overdrive and Mary were at the kitchen table getting caught up on the books, when Lizzie Flint came cantering into the yard. They exchanged smiles, as Lizzie tied her thoroughbred to an apple tree in the orchard, hunted windfall apples, and tossed them within reach of her steed. Then, Lizzie started toward the house, and Mary met her at the door.

Flush-faced and hair askew, Lizzie gushed, "Hi Mrs. Evans. I just couldn't let a day like this pass without going for a ride. Hope I'm not interrupting."

Mary beamed at the sight of her, "Oh goodness no, Lizzie. Come in, come in. Mr. Evans and I were just getting caught up on some paperwork."

Lizzie shyly flashed Overdrive a smile, "Hi. Beautiful day, isn't it?"

Overdrive smiled back, "Indeed it is. Have a seat ... please."

Mary asked, "Can I get you anything? There's some leftover apple pie, would you like a piece?"

Lizzie shook her head, "No thanks, but a glass of water would be nice."

As she fetched the water, Mary said over her shoulder, "I'm not sure you know, but Jumbo's at basketball practice."

Lizzie nodded, "Yes, I know all about it. Most of the team also played football, so after the deep run into the playoffs, Coach Mild is trying to whip them into basketball shape." She paused, and gestured at the both of them, "I actually came to speak to you."

Eyebrows up, Overdrive and Mary shared a quick glance, and Mary said, "Okay, what can we do for you?"

Lizzie leaned forward, "Well, my brother's best friend has expressed an interest in getting to know Kathy. They'd been after me to bring her to a home football game, but I knew Kathy wasn't into football enough to put up with the cold. Now that it's basketball season, at least she'd be comfortable. But before mentioning any of this to Kathy, I thought it'd be best if we spoke first. She's only a sophomore, and I wasn't sure you wanted her dating yet."

Impressed, Overdrive said, "What can you tell us about this young man?"

Lizzie sipped her water, and said, "He comes from a good family, and he's a perfect gentleman. Like my brother, he's a junior though, if that's a problem."

Mary shook her head, "That wouldn't be a problem. And he sounds like a very nice young man." She paused, uncertain whether to continue, then said, "Unlike some others that've shown an interest in Kathy."

Lizzie's eyes narrowed, "I wasn't sure you'd been

aware of that. And I agree. This'd be a way of getting Kathy in with a better group of kids. And I'd be able to keep an eye on her, and help her make better choices."

Mary opened her mouth to reply, but before she could, Overdrive said, "That's an excellent idea, Lizzie. And we appreciate you coming to us and offering, we really do. Kathy's ... er ... direction, has been a big worry for us."

Lizzie smiled knowingly, "I thought it might be." She stood to leave, "I waved at Kathy and Marie as I rode in. What're they up to in the garden so late in the year?"

Mary looked that way, and said, "These last few days have thawed the surface. They're rototilling the organic waste into the soil and picking rocks, to make next spring a little easier."

On the way out the door, Lizzie said, "I'll go talk to Kathy. If she asks to go to the game Friday night, you'll know why."

Overdrive and Mary both watched as Lizzie put an extra bounce in her step, on her way to the garden. After a moment, Overdrive turned to Mary and said, "If Jumbo let's her get away, he's a fool." That evening Kathy asked permission to go to the basketball game on Friday night, and Overdrive and Mary were all for it.

* * *

Two months later, give or take, it's the last Saturday in January, and fouler weather would be hard to imagine. With the temperature at 25 F below zero and wind gusts to 30 mph, windchill was literally off the charts in the wrong direction. The sky was a nasty mix of dark and darker greys. None of that would've mattered, if the day could be spent indoors. But the first silo had run empty that morning, which meant the silo unloader needed to be relocated to the top of the second one, preferably before evening milking.

Just looking out the kitchen window made Overdrive shudder. Moving the silo unloader mid-winter was the ultimate shit job. Every year he swore he'd purchase a second unloader, so each silo would have its own. But without fail, one financial setback or another always got in the way, and last year was no exception. He perused the doleful view while finishing his breakfast coffee, and cursed under his breath. He could foresee how the day would go, and it wasn't pretty.

Mumbling to himself, Overdrive took his seat at the head of the table. Then, he cleared his throat to gain the attention of Old Bill and the boys, and said, "Listen up. Today we move the silo unloader." Overdrive turned to his oldest son, "Jumbo, you'll take it apart with help from grandpa and me. The cold plays games with memory, so let's bag all the fasteners and label the bags. Then, we'll hoist each piece to the top of the second silo. You'll be the goalie up top, pulling each piece in through the roof."

Through a phony grin, Jumbo cracked, "Lucky me."

Undeterred, Overdrive said, "You can't just unhook the pieces and toss them down onto the silage this year. Everything's brittle in the cold, and something might break. Instead, use the silo's suspension cable to lower them."

Jumbo thought about that, then said, "Okay, let's talk through how that'll work. A piece comes up on the hoist cable. I pull it in through the roof, snap on the silo's cable, and unhook the other one. Hmmm … that won't work. I can't even reach the silo's cable. It hangs straight down out in the middle."

Overdrive scratched his head, "True enough. You'll need a short trailer rope up there. Tie it to the silo's cable, and use it to tie the cable off to the side, where you can reach it. Then, after the piece is on the silo's cable, you can use the same rope to gently swing it to the center by meting out line. When the piece is dangling in the center, give us a wave outside, and we'll crank it down until it rests on the silage. Set the pieces around the perimeter up there, so the center's always clear to land the next piece."

Jumbo had a thought, "I see another problem. I'll need to lower myself onto the silage and then get back up to the roof opening. In previous years, I'd jump, but that won't be possible the way I'll be dressed today."

Overdrive nodded, "Good point, we'd better hoist a ladder up top."

Jumbo asked, "What're we hoisting with?"

Overdrive winked at Old Bill, and said, "Your grandpa and I borrowed Brock's tractor-mounted winch, so we won't have to fool with ropes and pulleys in this weather. To get us started, all you need to do is climb the outside of the silo with the end of the hoist cable, and a spool of rope. Thread the cable through the pulley up top, tie the rope to the end, and drop us the rope. We'll use it to pull the cable end down, and as the trailer rope when pieces are being winched up."

Jumbo frowned, "You want me to climb the outside of the silo? Won't I be frozen stiff by the time I get up there?"

Overdrive nodded his shared concern, "Well, it's colder than a witch's tit out there, I'll grant you that. But going up the outside is the only way to place the cable. You'll be fine if you dress right. Wear a balaclava under your fur-lined trapper's hat, and tuck it under your thermal underwear around the neck. Pull down the hat's ear flaps, and use the chin strap. There's plenty of room in those felt-lined Sorel boots, so wear two pairs of wool socks, one inside the long johns, one out. When you're done setting the cable, shelter inside the silo until we get the ladder up to you. Then you can use the ladder to get down onto the silage, and be inside the chute and out of the wind, for the climb down."

Jumbo's brow creased, "I'd love to, but the chute doors are in, and they can't be removed from inside the silo. Who's going to remove that top door?"

Overdrive turned to his second oldest son, "Joe, that'll be your job. Those door locks stick, so take WD-40 and a hammer up the chute with you. It won't be a wasted trip, because I need you to pitch the spoiled, frozen silage down the chute, anyway. Hmmm ... you'll need a silage fork and an ice pick. For the climb up, maybe dangle them from your waist with a rope. When tossing down the spoils, keep digging until you reach unfrozen good silage, and leave a level surface. When done, leave the tools up there, in case the unloader gets stuck during startup."

Joe replied unwisely, "Why do I always get all the shit jobs? It'll take hours to break up and toss down that shit. I'll probably freeze to death. And there's no way I can drag the fork and pick up the chute. The pick weighs a ton, and the fork will snag on every hand and foot hold."

Overdrive darkened, but Jumbo spoke first, "I'll be happy to trade jobs with you, Joe. Wouldn't want you to be treated unfairly. Come on, let's shake on it."

Joe recoiled, "Come on now big guy ... I mean ... that's not what I meant. You must've misunderstood. What I meant was ... er ... well, I sure as hell don't want your job. Get that paw away from me."

Overdrive let him swing for a moment, then said, "Joe, wear your mitts and Sorels, and you'll be fine. Once you get to work, you'll be shedding layers to avoid breaking a sweat." Then he threw him a bone, "You might have a point with the fork and pick. We'll hoist them up the outside, along with the ladder."

Joe mumbled thank you, then after a moment said, "If it's like last year, there'll be so much waste it'll back up into the chute, if not cleared from below."

Overdrive nodded, and turned to John and David, "You boys need to clear the spoils. Keep your head clear, so you don't get knocked out by a falling chunk. Use the wheel barrow, dump it into the gutters, and spread it out. Every so often, run the barn cleaner so you don't have to wheel it so far. Remember to reposition the manure spreader before it spills over. Any questions?"

With deer-in-headlight looks, John and David's eyes met, then John said in a small voice, "I've never run the barn cleaner before. And the John Deere 70 is on the spreader. With the pony motor and all, I don't know how to start it."

Overdrive half-smiled at John's earnest foresight, "No problem. I'll show you how to run the barn cleaner. Come get me or Jumbo to start the 70."

John shrugged, "Okay, I guess me and the runt can clear the waste."

David protested, "I'm not a runt!"

Overdrive talked them through everything one last time, because mistakes could be deadly out in the cold. Hoisting involved them all, so this procedure was explained with great care. When finished, he looked around the table and everyone met his eyes, which he found encouraging.

*   *   *

The reality outside, as the Evans men headed to the barn, was even worse than the beast they'd imagined. The first wind gust sent them all scrabbling for purchase. To stay upright, they widened their stances, flexed at the knees and waist, took shorter steps, and leaned into the wind. As they tentatively navigated their way, each step emitted an other-worldly squeak, only to vanish into the gale. Each person's breath appeared as an intermittent plume trailing off downwind.

Simply reaching the barn felt like a noteworthy achievement. Crossing the threshold, the Evans men basked in the pungent warmth of the herd as if it were mana from heaven. John's glasses fogged instantly, and he accidently stepped on the heel of one of his brothers, and stumbled onto the freshly-limed concrete as they walked the center aisle toward the silos. Overdrive gave him a hand up, and then fell in behind him for fear he'd veer into a shit-filled gutter. When they exited the far end of barn, the fogged lenses turned into frosted ones, and John nearly headered straight into a silo before Overdrive grabbed his arm.

Outside once more, Jumbo initiated his miserable climb, while Overdrive and Old Bill meted out the winch cable. As a show of moral support, Overdrive felt it important for the others to watch, rather than cower in the barn. Huddling together for warmth failed, so he told Joe to fire up the tractor that would later power the winch, and they all herded to the leeward side of the engine block. This proved beneficial if tall, but John and

David still caught direct wind from under the block, so Overdrive sent them to the barn with David serving as the seeing-eye.

As Overdrive watched Jumbo climb, he imagined he could see him stiffen as he went, and considered calling the whole thing off. But soon Jumbo reached the height where an open cage surrounded the ladder the rest of the way up, and Overdrive shrugged off his doubts. After what seemed like an eternity, Jumbo finally reached the top. Mitts and winter gear made threading the cold-stiffened cable through the pulley a challenge, but soon it was done and the trailer rope came tumbling down. When Jumbo waved, Overdrive sent Joe into the barn to climb the chute, and open the top chute door.

Meanwhile, Overdrive and Old Bill quickly pulled the cable-end back to ground, and hooked on a bundle that included the fork, pick and ladder. Overdrive let his father run the winch controls, while he manned the trailer rope to hold the bundle away from the silo on the way up. Both men peered upward as the items rose. Jumbo had cracked open the silo roof, and crawled inside to get out of the wind. But occasionally, he peeked out to see the progress of the ascending load. When it neared the top, Jumbo waved and Old Bill eased the load to a stop.

A moment elapsed, while Jumbo pulled the items in through the roof, unhooked them, and tossed them down onto the frozen silage. Then Jumbo waved for Overdrive to pull the cable-end back to ground, and ducked back inside the roof and out of the frigid gale.

* * *

Blinded by frosted glasses, John tripped and fell as

he raced outside to his father. In a panicked voice, he shouted, "Dad, Jumbo's passed out! Joe shouted down the chute for help. When he got up top and popped open the top door, Jumbo was just lying there!"

Overdrive tossed the trailer rope in Old Bill's direction, and broke into a dead run. Over his shoulder, he shouted, "Dad, pull the cable-end down and snap it to a stave. Then come inside. John, get back in the barn."

Mind racing, Overdrive hustled through the barn door and around the corner to the second silo's chute. Under it stood David, in shock. Overdrive panted, "David, run to the house and tell your mom to call an ambulance. It might be exposure! Hell, it might even be silage gas!"

David took off running, as John and Old Bill huffed their way around the corner, "Where's David going ... what happened?"

Overdrive shook his head, "David's telling Mary to call an ambulance. I'm not sure what happened, probably exposure or silage gas. Either way, he'll be gone before the ambulance arrives, if we don't get him down and into the warm barn."

Old Bill's eyebrows shot up, "Get him down? How?"

Already scrambling up the chute, Overdrive yelled back, "I don't know yet, but we've got to."

When half way up, Overdrive heard Joe shout in panic, "Dad, hurry! I don't know what to do!"

As he raced upward, Overdrive shouted, "I'm coming!"

Joe, a moment later, in a subdued voice, "Hurry, I'm feeling groggy too."

That news set Overdrive on fire, and he hurled himself upward with all his might. Scrabbling from handhold to foothold, arms and legs pumping, he screamed, "Joe, stand up! Stand up, son! NOW! And pull Jumbo up, too. Silo gas is heavier than air! You've got to get up!"

A moment later Overdrive shot out of the chute door to find Joe in a squat, straddling Jumbo and straining, with Jumbo's heft pinned to the wall in a sitting position. Joe cried, "I'm sorry Dad, I couldn't lift him."

Overdrive sprung forward, grabbed Joe under the arm pits, and shot him upright into a standing position. Voice breaking, he whispered into Joe's ear, "You did good, son." Then, urgently, "Now brace your legs and lean into the wall. I've got to let go, and get Jumbo."

Overdrive straddled Jumbo, wound himself into a deep crouch, and threaded his forearms under his son's armpits to hook them with his elbows. Then, with back straight, he used the large muscles of his legs to shoot upward with all his might. He strained as long as he dared, and achieved movement, but not much. Next, he repositioned and shot upward again, and gained a foot. Face-to-face now with his pale and unconscious first born, Overdrive summoned everything he had once more, and the adrenalin rushed in. He repositioned one last time, took the deepest breath of his entire life, and with a feral beast roar, shot upward and willed himself never to stop. With this last desperate burst, Overdrive managed to slide Jumbo up the wall to a standing position, just as his air gave out.

Joe sobbed, "Is he alright?"

Huffing and dizzy, Overdrive gasped, "He's breathing. I can see his breath. But he's still unconscious, so he's not out of the woods. How about you?"

Joe used his sleeve to wipe his eyes and nose, "I feel much better. The air must be okay up here."

Overdrive stared at him, evaluating, "Are you sure? It's important."

Joe nodded, "Ah-huh, I'm fine now. Really."

Satisfied, Overdrive said, "Okay. Come over here and help me position Jumbo's legs, so they can hold some of his weight. Take a deep breath and hold it, then go down and spread his legs to about shoulder width. That's it, good. Now stand back up and breathe. Okay, now take another deep breath, and go down and pull each heal about a foot from the wall. That's a boy, now stand and breathe. I can't see, are his legs locked straight?"

Joe looked down, "Yup."

Overdrive looked both ways, "Okay, now step in here and see if you can hold him up. That's it, come right in under me. Keep him pressed hard against the wall. Have you got him?"

Joe grunted, "Yeah, I've got him."

Overdrive let go, stepped over to the chute, peered down, and yelled, "Dad, are you down there?"

Old Bill shouted back, "Yes … along with John."

Overdrive, in an urgent tone, "Okay. John, listen to me closely. Go get a five-or-six-foot log chain from the machine shed, wrap it around your neck, and climb up here as fast as you can. Run son! Run like the wind!" John threw his useless glasses to the side and took off.

A moment later David returned with Mary, and she shouted up the chute, "How's Jumbo? The ambulance is on its way."

Overdrive shouted, "Jumbo's breathing but unconscious. It's silo gas for sure, but maybe the cold too. If we can keep him standing, he can breathe fresh air. Joe and I have him propped up against the wall, in a standing position."

Mary's voice cracked, "Oh my god! How long did he breathe the gas? That can be ..." She glanced at Old Bill and David, and refrained from saying *fatal*.

Mind sharp, Overdrive snapped, "Stay focused on what we need to do! Where the hell is John! I need that chain!"

Old Bill shouted, "He's running up the aisle toward us. Be here in a second."

Overdrive barked, "Get out of his way. He needs to get up here fast!"

Soon, the clinking noise of John's ascension began. Old Bill shouted over the din, "Son, you need to tell us the plan. What's the chain for?"

Overdrive shouted back, "Jumbo's too big to sling over my back and come down the chute. We'll have to winch him down the outside. He's heavy and awkward, and we'd never be able to get him up the ladder to the roof opening. We'll need to use the silo's cable to pull him up, with you on the hand-crank down there. Once we get him up, we'll put him on the outside winch cable. Another problem is, we can't just wrap these cables around him under the arms, and hook them back on themselves. It'd be like a heavy weight on a choke chain, and we'd crush his chest. That's what the chain is for."

Old Bill thought about that, then shouted, "Okay, I got that part, but we've got another problem. Outside, the cable-end is hooked to a stave at ground level. Mary can handle the crank in here. I'll run out there and winch the cable-end back to the top, along with the rope. Don't forget to tie the trailer rope to Jumbo's feet."

Overdrive winced, "Shit! With Joe and John up here, who's going to handle the trailer rope? David can't do it alone."

Mary shouted, "I'll help him."

Overdrive scoffed, "You're not dressed for it. You'll freeze out there."

Mary shouted back, "I'll send David to fetch my warm gear. The girls know where it is. They'll also watch for the ambulance, and direct them to the barn."

The whole family sprang into action. Mary manned the crank on the silo's cable. With her providing the lift, Overdrive, Joe and John managed to wrestle Jumbo's heft to the catwalk outside. By then, Old Bill had winched the cable-end back up top. Without delay, Overdrive and his two sons switched Jumbo to the outside cable, tied the trailer rope to his feet, and dropped it below. By the time it fell to the ground, Mary was there in her warmest gear, along with David. With them manning the trailer rope, Jumbo up top was moved to a dangling position free of interference, and Old Bill began lowering him with the winch.

Once Jumbo was off to a snag-free start, Overdrive herded Joe and John back in through the silo's roof, down the ladder onto the silage, and into the chute for the climb down. When Jumbo reached the ground, Overdrive, Joe and John were there to carry him into the barn, with Mary and David racing ahead to hold open the barndoors. When Jumbo crossed the threshold into the warmth of the barn, medics were thirty yards away, coming down the center aisle at a dead run.

Silo gas, also known as nitrogen dioxide, was a familiar risk in America's Dairyland, which meant the medics knew exactly what to do. Within seconds, Jumbo was on oxygen. Within minutes, he'd been transported by stretcher into the ambulance. Overdrive rode with his son in the back of the ambulance, to the ER at Plymouth

Hospital. Mary followed in the family car. Old Bill, Joe, John, David, Kathy, and Marie stood in the back yard, and watched them go.

* * *

After spending the rest of the day at the hospital, Overdrive and Mary pulled into the farm's yard after dark, about a half hour later than the normal start-time for milking. As he drove in, Overdrive noticed fresh tractor tracks in the snow, headed around the barn to the land beyond. Once parked, a despondent Mary went to the house, but Overdrive investigated further. Telltale droppings, visible in the dim light, told him the manure spreader had been taken out back, and apparently unloaded. Given the foul weather, and the fact that only he and Jumbo knew how to start the John Deere 70, this surprised him. Curious now, he walked to the manure spreader bay at the end of the barn, and turned on the light. There sat the 70 and spreader, over half-filled again with spoiled silage.

The barn lights were on, so Overdrive headed inside. As he entered, his ears were greeted by the whir of the vacuum pump, and at the far end of the barn, the sounds of the milking machines it powered. Huh … sounded like somebody's milking. Skeptical, he glanced around and was stunned to find each cow contentedly chewing its evening ration of silage. How's that even possible?

Dumbfounded, Overdrive stepped to the center aisle, and fast-walked toward the sound of the milking machines. By the time he got there, everyone in the barn had dropped their tasks to gather around. Clearly not himself, Overdrive seemed not to understand why everyone was staring at him. Old Bill broke the awkward silence by asking, "How's Jumbo?"

On the first try at responding, Overdrive's voice cracked, and he had to stop. When ready, he tried again, "He's stable and awake, and they say he's going to be fine. They want to keep him overnight for observation." Shaken, he continued in an anguished voice, "It'd been foolish to try to move the unloader on a day like today. My foolishness, almost got him ... oh my god ..."

Old Bill stepped forward and embraced his son, who gave in and sobbed openly. The older man whispered, "Hey, listen to me ... It's alright son. Jumbo's going to be fine. You said so yourself."

Joe, John and David had never seen their father cry before, and didn't know what to do. Grandpa swung his head for them to join, so the boys stepped up and wrapped their arms. Eventually, Overdrive regained his composure, cleared his throat, and asked, "How'd you feed silage without an unloader?"

Joe said proudly, "I broke up the frozen spoil on top of the silo, and tossed it down the chute."

John piped up, "David and I threw the spoils into the gutter. When Joe reached good silage up top, he climbed down to help."

David added, "Every time we wanted the barn cleaner to move, I ran up the aisle to tell Gramps, and he did it."

Eyes twinkling, Old Bill continued, "When it came time to move the spreader, Joe and I figured out how to crank up the 70."

Joe beamed, "The barn cleaner hadn't been run yet today, so the gutters were full to begin with. Between the cow shit and silo spoils, I had to empty the spreader twice before all the spoils were cleared. Then I climbed back up the silo, and threw enough good silage down to feed the herd."

Overdrive looked from one proud smiling face to another, shook his head in mock disbelief, then asked, "Who's doing the milking?"

Old Bill poked a finger into his son's chest, and said, "I am, you dummy. Who do you think taught you? In fact, tonight I taught John how, and he picked it up faster than you ever did. We've had to alternate carrying the milk pails, and that's slowed us down a little. But other than that, it's going fine."

David piped up, "I'll carry the milk, after I finish feeding the calves."

Joe patted him on the back, "Actually, little brother, you're not big enough to carry the milk. I'll do it, after I've finished feeding the hay. But Davie, it'd be a big help if you kept the hay pushed up in the mangers, so the cows can reach it."

David bobbed his head, "I can do that."

Old Bill said wisely, "Look son, you've had enough excitement for the day. Why don't you go to the house? Kathy and Marie have dinner waiting for you, and Mary might need a little company about now. Don't worry about the milking, we've got it covered."

CHAPTER 12

The Evans's Vow Never Again – Sunday;
January 31, 1965; 10:00 AM

After breakfast on the day after the accident, and still shaken by the near loss of his oldest son, Overdrive asked Joe and John to winch an electric fan and extension cord to the top of the second silo. Then, Overdrive climbed the chute, set up the fan, and cleared any remaining silo gas himself. Having learned his lesson, he decided to delay the unloader move until the weather broke. In the interim, twice daily, Joe manually threw down enough silage to feed the herd.

The weather didn't break until the following Thursday, when the kids were in school. While waiting for a reasonable day to come along, Overdrive had managed to disassemble the unloader in the first silo, by working for short spurts in the frigid cold.

On the day of the move, it was sunny, the wind was still, and temperatures rose above freezing. Overdrive and Old Bill carried the pieces outside and dropped them near the winch. Then Overdrive climbed up top to play goalie, while Mary manned the trailer rope, and Old Bill ran the winch with one hand and helped Mary with the other.

Shorthanded and under the gun to finish the move before the weather turned wicked again, Overdrive simply unhooked the pieces up top, and tossed them down onto the silage. The silage was unfrozen, and luckily, nothing had been badly broken. Sure, the auger shield had dented and its brackets had bent, but after a few whacks with the rubber mallet they'd been straightened well enough not to rub.

Overdrive had to scramble all day, but he did manage to reassemble the unloader before dinner time. Of course, when he first pushed the on-button, nothing happened. Though tempted to kick the shit out of it, he refrained from doing so. After a quick diagnostic check, he found the emergency cutoff switch had been inadvertently flipped during the move. With the issue resolved, he stepped back in satisfaction when the unloader came to life on the second try.

* * *

Overdrive and Mary mutually decided not to speak about Jumbo's accident immediately, giving each other a chance to process the experience independently, and in their own way. Early on, Overdrive repressed any thought of it altogether. Just thinking about it, overwhelmed him with guilt. Instead, he busied himself with the unloader move and catching up on other chores. He reasoned the move had to be top priority, since feeding silage manually wasn't sustainable.

Over time, Overdrive worked up the courage to think about what had happened. In his view, if Jumbo had died it would've been his fault, and that fact was hard to live with. Yes, the attempt to move the unloader on that blustery frigid day had been foolhardy. But even worse, the danger of silo gas had completely slipped his mind. Joe may very well have saved Jumbo's life. Whenever the thought surfaced that both sons might've been lost, Overdrive did his best to beat it back into his subconsciousness.

One day while pondering what'd happened, Overdrive had an epiphany. Every year, right after a silo was filled, he always made sure the top chute door was removed, and the silo's roof door opened. Doing so, meant any silo gas would naturally-vent away. This year, he'd been distracted by HMR's bombshell and the fight to save the farm, and had forgotten to vent that second silo. He hadn't mis-planned the unloader move … well, except for going ahead on such a wicked day. Instead, he'd failed to vent the silo right after it'd been filled.

Overdrive forced himself to envision a future without Jumbo, and didn't like what he saw. For Overdrive, it'd always been about being a good steward of the farm, and passing it along within the family. With six children, he'd always felt upbeat about his chances. But the accident had forced him to think deeper, and see a different reality. The odds of keeping the farm in the family were far slimmer than he'd been assuming. Yes, there were five other kids. But upon closer examination, none of them were as suited to take over as Jumbo.

Jumbo was a mountain of a man, and up to any of the physical demands of farming. He's also smart enough to handle the required mental gymnastics, and unusually gifted in the operation of heavy equipment. Joe has made strides in the past year, but by demeanor, remains more inclined to whine than put his shoulder to the harness and lead. John is book-smart, and may have better options than farming. David's so young, it's hard to tell where he might come out.

Mary insisted he shouldn't forget about Kathy and Marie, but Overdrive had a hard time seeing either of them running the farm. He supposed that having Joe as a hired hand might help, presuming they'd get along. It's certainly possible one or the other girl might marry someone, so together they'd have the capacity and inclination, but that seemed like a longshot. No, Jumbo was the best bet.

Overdrive refocused on the underlying problem … two silos, but only one unloader. They'd been meaning to get another unloader for years. But time and again, something would come up, and they wouldn't have the money. The move between silos had always fallen mid-winter, when weather was at its very worst. It was a pain in the ass, but on a farm, lots of tasks fell into that category. Out of necessity, there's a tendency to just shrug and soldier on. Perhaps his senses had become dulled to the danger, but if so, the accident had solved that problem.

Bottom line, acquiring another unloader would take money. Unfortunately, this boiled down to the price of raw milk, which dairy farmers currently had no say in. In his mind, the best bet for changing that was the NFO. Toward that end, next week at the February meeting, there'd be a vote on whether the Sheboygan County NFO should launch a market intervention. Under the proposed plan, beverage milk would be diverted to a local cheese factory. The timing of the diversion, starting a week after the vote, seemed right. It coincided with the time of year when raw beverage milk was in shortest supply. The diversion would continue, until the original processor signed an agreement with the NFO, resetting the price paid to farmers for raw milk at a higher level.

For the milk diversion to be successful, the farmers behind it would need staying power. To make that possible, the NFO had already signed an agreement with the local cheese factory. Generally, milk for cheese fetched less than milk for beverage, but the factory's new owner agreed to pay a premium to jumpstart his business. In addition, the NFO's national organization offered to collect the farmer's milk and haul it to the cheese factory for free, whereas previously, the farmers had been paying the freight. With the net milk price to farmers essentially staying the same, the NFO was confident they'd have enough leverage to force the original processor to negotiate in good faith, and come to a reasonable agreement.

The NFO's proposal had been introduced at the previous month's meeting, and Overdrive and Mary had been kicking it around in their heads ever since. They hadn't yet decided to vote in favor of the diversion, but neither saw any flaws and both thought the plan had a reasonable chance for success. Before next week's meeting, they needed to figure out where they stood.

During milking the following morning, Mary dropped hints that she was ready to talk about Jumbo's accident. Overdrive used the opportunity to remind her they also needed to make a decision on the NFO vote. They made plans to head to Harbor Lights after the evening milking, to discuss both topics.

✻ ✻ ✻

At Harbor Lights, Overdrive and Mary walked into a larger than usual crowd. Some of the winners of last weekend's Lake Ellen Ice Fishing Jamboree were there, regaling their friends with tales of their exploits. The fish in the photos didn't look nearly as large as those being described, but everybody seemed to be having a good time. They joined the fun for a while, but then slunk away with their beers to a table in a quiet corner.

Mary leaned forward and whispered, "To begin with, I need to get something off my chest." Then, she sat up straight and looked him in the eye, "James, what were you thinking, trying to move the unloader on a day like that?"

Overdrive, contrite, "It was stupid, Mary. I know that now."

Mary pointed a finger at him, and snarled, "Stupid, you're God-damned right it was stupid. You could've gotten Jumbo killed!"

Overdrive, with genuine remorse, "I know, I know. It was bone-headed, and I apologize. But it wasn't the cold, it was the silo gas."

Mary rose up to lunge at him, thought better of it, and sat back down. After a moment to calm herself, "Silo gas. Thanks for bringing that up. What the hell, James! How long have you been farming? What happened!"

Overdrive held up his hands in a placating gesture, "Look, I'm sorry, okay. I apologized. Please let me explain." He took a deep breath, and said in a contrite voice, "Every year when we finish filling a silo, I make sure we take out the top chute door and crack open the silo's roof, so any silo gas vents away. This year, after HMR gave us 30 days to pay up or get out, I got distracted and forgot to vent that second silo. It's my fault, Mary, and I'm sorry."

Mary opened her mouth to reply, but paused to let that sink in. Possibly mollified, she nodded, "Well, we did have a lot on our minds back then." Then, she said in a soft voice, "But Jumbo could've been killed."

Overdrive reached out, put his hand on Mary's, and looked her in the eye, "I know honey. I know." He squeezed her hand, and held it for the longest time. Then he said, "I need to get something off my chest, too."

Mary searched his eyes, "I'm listening."

Overdrive continued to hold her hand, "After Joe found Jumbo, I shot up the chute as fast as I could. While on the way, Joe shouted down that he felt groggy, too. That's when I knew for sure it was silo gas. I shouted for him to stand up, and pull Jumbo up too, if he could. Mary, we could've lost them both."

Mary gasped, "Oh my god!"

Still holding hands, Overdrive continued, "Joe was able to get Jumbo sitting upright against the wall, probably saved his life." Visibly shaken now, he said, "I don't think … I'd … I'd never have forgiven myself, if we'd lost either one."

They sat in silence holding hands, each lost in their own thoughts. Neither knew what to say. Finally, Mary offered him a tiny smile, and said, "Joe helped, but it's your quick thinking that saved Jumbo. The doctor said as much."

Overdrive shook his head, "It took us all to save Jumbo. It's a miracle we got him down out of that silo in time. A miracle, plain and simple."

Mary nodded, "I guess the lord helps those who help themselves. At least the first time. After that, we're supposed to learn our lesson." She thought a moment, then said, "James, what're we going to do? We can't let that happen again, ever."

Overdrive said solemnly, "We need to buy another unloader."

Mary looked down, "We've been saying that for years, but spending money that way never seems to make the cut."

Serious now, Overdrive said, "It all boils down to money, which means the price of raw milk. We need to vote yes on that NFO milk diversion proposal."

Mary looked at him for a moment, then lowered her voice, "I agree. We got where we are by taking whatever they'll give us. We can't keep living this way."

CHAPTER 13

Rachel's Personal Bests – Monday;
November 9, 1964; 6:00 AM

After deciding to relive her two most life-changing experiences at Wolf's Run, Rachel enjoyed a restful sleep. The next morning, she was up at the crack of dawn. When she sauntered into the dining room, the housekeeper appeared instantly with coffee and breakfast. Rachel asked the woman to pack her a lunch and thermos of hot cocoa, and separately, to slice and pack the remaining raw ribeye steak. The latter was an odd request, but the housekeeper simply nodded, having learned long ago never to question the boss lady.

As she worked her way through breakfast, Rachel noticed a growing anticipation. It was a welcome relief, caring again, for what the day might hold. When the housekeeper returned, they had a back-and-forth over the evening's dinner menu, and for her cocktail, Rachel requested a Bobby Burns using the 12-year-aged Chivas Regal blended scotch. Rachel shared when she could be expected to return, and they settled on a time for dinner to be on the table. After finishing her coffee, Rachel rose, stowed the lunch and other items in her backpack, donned her coat and gear, and stepped out into the wilderness.

As planned, Rachel started her excursion by hiking her favorite trails. The hikes, in addition to a physical warmup, provided time to review and refresh her memory on the backstory for the day's reenactment. Today she'd relive a special day from her life as a first-grader. Even at that age, Rachel enjoyed hiking the grounds by herself, silently taking in the sights, sounds, and smells. Yes, she enjoyed seeing the wildlife, but what fascinated her most were the feral cats, and how they interacted with her father.

Generations ago, the family had brought cats to the estate to keep the rodents down in the outbuildings. Over the years, they multiplied, but were generally out of sight and mind. The estate had a dock on the Menominee River, and Rachel's Dad used to clean his fish there. To dispose of the waste, he'd pound the butt end of his filleting knife on the dock, and to Rachel's astonishment, soon there'd be cats everywhere. Dad always had plenty to go around, but they'd scrabble for the fish guts anyway, which angered her father no end. Sometimes he'd try to break up the fights with an oar, but the cats never paid much attention, so he invariably ended up walking off in disgust.

Rachel was always curious about how things would turn out, and liked to stay behind to see the endgame. On more than one occasion, she'd seen cats injured and unable to reach cover, at least fast enough to matter. They'd either lay there bleeding on the bank, or futilely try to drag themselves away. On these occasions, Rachel would step off a safe distance back into the woods, and find a comfortable sitting place from which to watch. She'd been proud of her ability to sit silently and observe, at such a young age. Usually, lone coyotes would gobble up the injured cats, but once an entire wolfpack swooped in and fought with each other over the spoils. That'd been awesome!

So it was, that one day Rachel was out for a walk, soon after a storm with high winds had passed. She loved the fragrance that came with the rain. As she walked along, she spied a bird's nest that had fallen out of a tree. In and around it, were five baby birds, peeping and cartwheeling helplessly. Rachel walked up and stooped low on her haunches to get a better look, and consider their predicament. While trying to decide what to do, incessant squawking broke her concentration. Over her shoulder, she observed what must've been the mother bird, alternately dive-bombing or landing nearby, feigning a broken wing. Rachel remembers thinking ... *mommy bird was definitely not happy.*

Soon, Rachel had an idea that brought a smile to her face. She bent low, picked up the nest, rounded up the scattered hatchlings, and placed them inside. Then she made her way toward the dock, with the squawking mother-bird never far behind. Rachel scanned the ground intently as she walked along, and stooped carefully to pick up the perfect rock, when she found it. The going was slow with both hands full, but eventually she reached the dock. While holding the nest with squirming hatchlings carefully against her chest, Rachel pounded the rock on the dock, and then waited.

Sure enough! In no time, Rachel was surrounded by feral cats. She gently lifted one of the hatchings out of the nest, and tossed it out among them to see what would happen. Such a ruckus she'd never witnessed before. All she could do was stand there in awe. Fragmented memories returned ... cat hair flying ... mother-bird zooming in and out ... blood and feathers everywhere. When it ended, the dominant cat ran off with what remained of the peeper. The rest circled and eyed each other, growling threats. Well, except for the one trying to drag itself away.

Mesmerized, Rachel repeated her jump-ball maneuver with the remaining hatchlings, noting with clinical precision the various outcomes. When done, there'd still only been one cat down, a fact she took as disappointing. She shooed away the hangers-on, which were scuffed up but still on their feet. Then, she carefully stepped back into the woods, and settled into a comfortable hidey hole to enjoy the show. As she'd hoped, her patience had again been rewarded. Suddenly an eagle swooped in, then beat its way back into the sky. Rachel dashed into a clearing to get a better look. As the eagle ascended, she could clearly see the cat dangling from its talons, still kicking and yowling. Rachel remembers being gape-mouthed and speechless, gazing up into the sky and thinking ... *Wow! This is the best day ever! Who says cats can't fly?*

Having completed her warm up, Rachel next visited the exact spot where she'd found the nest, all those years ago. In her mind, she could see the hatchlings on the ground and see, hear, and smell the terror of the mother bird. Her nape-hairs rose, and that old familiar tingling feeling began. After taking a moment to enjoy the sensation, Rachel walked to the exact spot where she'd picked up the rock. She spied another much like the one from years ago, picked it up, and walked to the dock.

There, she pounded the rock on the dock, and waited. When the cats appeared, she tossed them raw ribeye scraps one slice at a time, and enjoyed the show. As the pleasant sensations returned, Rachel thought ... *God, I love it here!*

* * *

The following day, after settling with the housekeeper the details for cocktail time and dinner, Rachel set off once more. This day's agenda would follow her tried-and-true routine, and involve reliving a special day from her life as a high-school junior. She'd always been especially proud of this one, since it'd taken her almost a full year to plan.

Rachel had grown up in a mansion near Sheboygan with her parents, Ben and Ruth, and brother Max. One weeknight during her sophomore year, brother Max, a freshman at the time, had gone to a friend's house after dinner to work on a class project. Rachel had gone upstairs to her room to study, and Rachel's parents had adjourned to the back patio. Not long after, Rachel heard arguing, and tiptoed down the hall to the upstairs sitting room, which overlooked the patio. She cracked a window to hear, and discovered Ruth in the process of dressing down Ben. While Rachel listened, her mother dredged up a long list of indignities she'd apparently suffered at the hands of her father. Some pre-dated their marriage, while others continued to this day.

Rachel struggled mightily to stifle her laughs at Ruth's litany of petty gripes, until one came along that struck a deep nerve. Apparently, Ben and Ruth had agreed to have only one child. But when it turned out to be a girl,

Rachel, Ben forced Ruth to risk her hourglass figure once more, hoping for a boy to carry on the family business. All these years later, Ruth remained furious over being treated, in her words, like a glorified brood mare. After Max was born, Ben's tubes were tied at Ruth's insistence, but the damage had already been done. She'd never recovered her maiden form, felt like a matronly frump, it'd all been Ben's fault, and so on.

The news had shocked Rachel. But upon hearing it, suddenly past happenings now made sense that she'd never fully understood before. Ben spent long hours with Max in his study, behind a closed and locked door. Rachel had always wondered what that was all about. Max wouldn't tell her initially, but over time she wore him down and he spilled his guts. That's how Rachel learned that the family business involved separating honest, hardworking people ... *suckers and losers* ... as Ben liked to call them, from their money, hopes, and dreams.

The more Rachel pieced together the truth, the angrier she became. She's smarter than Max by a light-year, and also beat him on any other credible measure of merit. Yet he's the one Ben was grooming to take over the family business. The twit even had the gall to lord that fact over her. In Rachel's view, by birthright the business should come to her. Having a pecker was the only reason Max had been chosen over her, and that wasn't right.

Rachel had been queen bee of her class throughout middle school. High school was the confluence of several middle schools, so as a freshman she'd expected stiff competition, but within a month had easily asserted her dominance. By junior year, Rachel's clique of popular girls was a well-oiled machine for doing her bidding. The cool guys all flocked to Rachel, and her minions orbited closely, hoping to be noticed themselves. To increase their odds, they dressed, walked, and even tried to talk like her. When Rachel made a suggestion, her girls heard it as an order. They knew if they didn't, Rachel would ignore or exclude them, or target them with one of her cruel pranks.

With a plan in mind, Rachel started grooming one of her minions, Millie, to serve as carnal bait for Max. Millie initially objected on the grounds that dating a sophomore would be humiliating, Rachel's brother or not. But Rachel gave her an offer she couldn't refuse. Millie would become Rachel's number two for the duration of high school. As part of the deal, Millie agreed that Rachel would bring she and Max together, and direct how the relationship would develop. Rachel made it clear that Millie would follow her directions exactly, or else. If she and Max were seen together by anyone, or if she had any communication with Max outside of Rachel-arranged encounters, Rachel swore she'd make Millie's life a living hell.

With Millie on board, Rachel set out to recruit Max. Millie was about the same height and weight as Rachel, and one of the hottest girls in school, so enlisting Max's participation wasn't much of a problem. Rachel simply fed him a line of bullshit about Millie having a crush on him, but him being younger and all, she couldn't be seen around school with him. Instead, Millie wanted Rachel to be their go-between. Max bought it, so Rachel arranged a series of private encounters between he and Millie, starting in late fall and on into winter.

In advance of each encounter, Rachel instructed Millie on how far to let Max go. She made it clear that Max told her everything, so if Millie failed to do her part,

Rachel would know. In accordance with Rachel's plan, the sessions between Max and Millie slowly escalated from talking only, to that plus innocent bumps and touches, to that plus tentative kissing and innocent caressing, to that plus deep kissing and light petting, to that plus heavy petting outside the clothing, and so on.

While all this was going on, Rachel observed her brother with a detached, almost clinical, curiosity as he went about his life between the increasingly heated encounters with Millie. As time went on, Max's reaction to the mere mention of Millie's name evolved markedly. Growing more frequent, were blush-faced episodes requiring him to finagle with his clothing, to free his privates from snags as he stiffened. Rachel used these and other signs to pace the next rendezvous, and determine how far to let Millie go during it. In short, her plan was working to perfection, as she knew it would.

Through careful manipulation of her star-crossed puppets, Rachel was able to peak Max's lust a few days before school broke for the Christmas holidays. Now any mention of Millie's name elicited heavy breathing, in addition to the telltale bulge, and whatnot. On que, Rachel laid out a story she'd been rehearsing for months. She told Max that Millie couldn't stand it anymore, that she needed to spend a night with him. Millie's family would be heading to their vacation home up north on Lundgren Lake Friday night, and staying there for the holidays. Millie had already gotten permission to drive the short distance to Wolf's Run, for a sleepover with Rachel on Saturday night. According to Rachel, Millie had begged her to figure a way to get Max there alone.

As the story unfolded, a shine came to Max's eyes, his heavy breathing quickened, and he began gushing ideas on how to get to Wolf's Run without their parents. Seeing these giveaways, Rachel knew she had him hooked. She already had a plan for getting Max to Wolf's Run, of course, but she wanted Max to think it'd been his idea so he'd sell it to their parents. With a little artful puppeteering, Rachel managed to get Max to see that his best bet was for Rachel to drive him, being that he's only 15 and without a driver's license.

Rachel knew it'd take some convincing for Ben and Ruth to allow them to take such a long road trip alone, in the dead of winter. But she'd already concocted a story she knew would carry the day, so she set about pulling Max's strings so he'd see it as his own. Soon, Max was advocating to Ben and Ruth that he and Rachel needed to get away and unwind from the pressures of their semester-ending final exams. He suggested if they went to Wolf's Run, they'd be able to do their parents a big favor. Since the whole family had been planning to go there anyway, the following week, by going early he and sis could chop the wood, clear the windfall branches, and whatnot before Ben and Ruth arrived.

The conversation with Ben and Ruth went as hoped. In fact, Rachel had been quite impressed with little brother's salesmanship. Apparently, he processed more quickly when thinking with his dick. Friday night came, and Rachel and Max left for Wolf's Run in one of the family's cars. During the drive, she primed him for what was to come. Max was aware that Millie had visited Rachel before at Wolf's Run, so he knew she'd be familiar with the lay of the land. Rachel leveraged this fact, to make her yarn about Millie's romantic fantasy seem more plausible.

As Rachel told it, Millie wanted to meet Max at the

bench overlooking the highest point of the river gorge. There, they'd sit together under the full moon, and enjoy the panoramic view of the Menominee River rapids, far below. After a little foreplay, she wanted to walk with Max hand-in-hand upstream along the moonlit river trail to the fishing shack at water's edge. In the fishing shack, in front of the flaming field-stone fireplace, was where Millie wanted to give herself to Max for the very first time. Millie said the beauty of the river at that location, where it widened and swirled slowly into a deep calm backwater, took her breath away.

After finishing her tall tale, Rachel risked a quick glance away from the road, and noted Max's eye-shine, flushed face, and labored breathing. For the rest of the drive, she smiled contentedly as Max prattled on, airing his ideas on how he'd prepare for the big night. How he'd swipe a bottle of Ben's best single-malt scotch whiskey and bring it to the shack, along with cut-glass crystal tumblers, ice, water, and snacks. How he'd lay in plenty of firewood, and set the fireplace ablaze in advance, so the shack would be toasty warm. How he'd clear an area in front of the fireplace, and put down a double-layer of foam pads, topped by zip-together sleeping bags and soft pillows. Toward the end he creepily babbled on about his vision of the scene, as he and Millie arrived at the shack … soft firelight bouncing all over the room, and so on. Rachel wanted to puke.

While on the road, Rachel and Max made stops for dinner, gas, and groceries and arrived late at Wolf's Run. Both tired, they fired up the heating system and went to bed. As she laid in bed, Rachel thought about Max's set-up for the fishing shack, and grudgingly had to admire how resourceful her dimwitted little brother became when motivated by sex. All that, from a twit that rarely managed to put on a pair of matching socks in the morning. She filed away the thought that perhaps this was true for any male, and drifted off to sleep.

In a deep dream-state, Rachel was lolling on a comfy raft enjoying the most perfect day when suddenly the glass-like seas turned into ferocious waves. Startled, she woke to find Max standing over her, with his hand rocking her shoulder. Her first thought, after realizing he couldn't wait for the day to start, was … *if only you knew*. Max literally bounced with anticipation, as Rachel tried to fix scrambled eggs and toast. Finally, she ordered him to sit before he broke something. Over breakfast, she teased him about the big night to come, then they planned their day.

As a security measure, their parents paid a local to plow the driveway whenever it snowed, to make it appear as if someone lived there. Hence, the heavy snow from a few days earlier had already been cleared. But it must've been windy since then, because they'd encountered snow drifts and windfallen branches during the previous night's drive in. Max wanted the estate to look its best for Millie's arrival, so he volunteered to clear the long, sinuous driveway. Rachel said she'd call Millie to firm up the timing details, and then whip up the food and gather the other provisions Max needed to prepare the fishing shack.

When Max returned, Rachel helped him backpack the gear out to the fishing shack. Along the way, she filled him in on the final details of Millie's fantasy. Millie wanted to wear her pink air force parka, with nothing but a teddy and jeans on underneath, and hike alone from the house to the river. She wanted the moon to be up and perfect, so she planned to arrive at the gorge at 6:00 PM, a little over an hour past dusk. She wanted Max to be standing near the bench at the overlook, waiting for her in the moonlight. As Rachel told it, Millie knew she wouldn't be able to hold back once she saw him. As a symbol of her sweet surrender, Millie wanted to run that last stretch and jump into Max's arms. With a touch of snark, Rachel suggested he better not drop her, if he wanted to get laid.

Soon, Rachel and Max arrived at the fishing shake and unloaded their packs. When Rachel left to head back to the house, Max was busily setting things up and exuding a lustful glow. During the hike, she pondered the design of the United States Air Force N-3B snorkel-hood parka. It had a full attached hood, which zipped right up, leaving only a small tunnel (or snorkel) out in front of the face, for the wearer to look out of. What a brilliant design for cold and windy weather, and how fortuitous that Millie owned an N-3B in hot pink.

Precisely at 6:00 PM the pink-clad figure emerged from the trail head and ran to her lover. When Max saw pink break from the thicket in the moonlight, his primal instincts kicked in. He bent slightly at the knees, held his arms in the catch position, and leaned forward for fear Millie's momentum would topple them backward into the snow. As she neared, she athletically hopped up, twisted, leaned back, and glided toward him horizontally. Face-up and left-side forward, she relaxed and feathered perfectly into Max's arms. Relieved that he hadn't dropped her, Max stood there for a moment, beaming goofily and swaying to regain his balance. When her right arm came whipping around toward his ear, he puckered up, assuming she's coming in for a kiss. Instead, the rock in her right hand crushed his left temple, and they fell in a heap.

The girl in pink struggled to her feet, dusted off the snow, unzipped and folded back the hood, and tossed her hair side-to-side. That girl was Rachel. She spent a moment studying her little brother, lying there on the ground. She'd done her homework, and surmised she'd crushed poor Max's pterion and ruptured his middle meningeal artery. He'd never survive the brain aneurism out here. Without delay, she bent down, grabbed his wrists, and dragged him to the cliff. Then she tossed him over and watched, as he bounced from rock to rock on the way to the rapids some 30 feet below. From there, he was swept away in the current.

Rachel took a moment to enjoy her great triumph. Everything had gone exactly as planned. There'd never been any rendezvous planned with Millie. In fact, Millie knew nothing of any of this. All she knew was that Rachel admired her pink parka. Back in November it'd been a birthday gift from Millie's grandfather, who'd been career USAF. He'd paid to have it custom made in Millie's favorite color, rather than the standard sage green. That parka was one of a kind.

Rachel had been puzzling over the details of her end game with Max for weeks, when one day Millie strutted into school wearing that pink parka. The moment Rachel saw it, the last puzzle piece fell into place. She marched right up to Millie, and slathered on the compliments. Not accustomed to the positive attention and defenses down, Millie said *of course* when Rachel asked if she could borrow it sometime. Well, that time had come.

In broad strokes, Rachel's plan had been designed to leave behind physical evidence suggesting that Max had inadvertently slipped and fallen off the cliff, and into the river to his death. But just to be safe, she surveyed the scene in the moonlight, with analytical precision. After a few finishing touches, such as scuffing away the drag marks in the snow, she hurried to the fishing shack. There, she quickly repacked everything that didn't belong. When done, she rearranged what remained to suggest the shack had been used by Rachel and Max to decompress from final exams, just as they'd told their parents. When satisfied, Rachel packed the gear back to the house in two trips, double-time.

Rachel wanted to be gasping for air and sobbing uncontrollably when she called her father. Lugging the gear made her breathless naturally, and she used her thespian skills for the rest. In an Oscar-worthy performance, she told the tale of spending the day with Max at the fishing shack, enjoying the fire and the beauty, Max begging to stay a bit longer, while Rachel returned to the house to prepare dinner, and then him never showing up.

Rachel, of course, had hiked back to the shack searching for him, but he hadn't been there. Frantic now, she called his name over and over, but no answer. Then, on the way back, she noticed his footprints in the snow, heading off the trail to the overlook. She went there and called out his name, but again, no answer. Then, in the moonlight, she saw what looked like disturbed snow down the bank to the river, as if he'd slipped and fallen in. In terror, she'd sprinted back to the house and called daddy. Totally taken in by Rachel's hysterics, Ben told his daughter to sit tight. He'd call the authorities, and then he and Ruth would be on their way.

When the call ended, Rachel sauntered into the bathroom and splashed cold water on her face. While drying, she studied herself in the mirror. She admired the rosy cheeks, and the eyes with that feral shine. She thought them quite becoming, in an exotic sort of way. When finished, she sashayed to the kitchen, filled her dinner plate, fetched a tall glass of water, and sat down to her evening meal. She'd prepared dinner before leaving the house in Millie's pink parka, and it'd been simmering on the stove ever since. She needed the used pots and pans to back up her story, so she left them undone in the sink to preserve physical evidence.

Rachel ate quickly and then hurried to stow the gear she'd packed back from the fishing shack. She wanted everything in its place when the authorities arrived. While stowing the gear, she made sure to continue to hydrate with water. Always thinking ahead, Rachel knew she'd have to conger another water-works performance when the cops arrived, and the tears had to come from somewhere.

Rachel played her role to perfection when the authorities arrived, and her encore for Mom and Dad was nothing short of masterful. Between sobs she contritely gurgled self-incriminations for leaving her little brother behind at the shack, failing to supervise him, not being there in his moment of need, and so on. While dealing with their own grief, Ben and Ruth consoled Rachel as best they could, and implored her to understand that it wasn't her fault, it was an accident. Poor, poor broken-hearted Rachel. My, how inconsolable she appeared to be.

With Max gone, Rachel became an only child again. Now unquestionably heir to the family business, since that day she'd been able to relax and savor her life of privilege as never before. She deftly played the part of the perfect daughter, as her parents grieved the loss of Max.

Rachel let her parents set the pace for when life would return to normal. After a respectful period, Ben inquired tentatively with Rachel, on whether she might have an interest in learning about the family business. Appearing humbled by the suggestion, Rachel replied if that's what'd make him happy, of course she would. Soon after, the secret sessions in the study resumed, only this time with Ben mentoring Rachel.

Pulling up and savoring these memories had consumed most of the day. Aside from lunch and a few potty breaks, Rachel had been hiking the entire time, and felt a satisfied glow from the exertion. Even so, she reserved plenty of time at the end of the day to relive events at the overlook. There, she'd nearly been overcome with sensation … nape hairs standing, tingling, first in the breasts and groin, then everywhere, and so on. As she hiked back to the main cabin, her mind dwelled on a thought … *You tried to steal my destiny, little brother. Big mistake!'*

* * *

After dinner, Rachel adjourned to the family room to enjoy a nightcap of Bailey's on the rocks, in front of the fireplace. One nightcap turned into two, as she noodled over whether she was fully rejuvenated. After much consideration, Rachel concluded she needed something more, but exactly what that was, eluded her. She kept noodling and finally, over the third nightcap, it dawned on her. Over time, everything had gone her way and she'd come to believe in her own invincibility. The casino setback had shaken that fundamental belief. The epiphany was simple … *To regain that sense of invincibility, she needed to relive ALL of the life experiences that'd given her that feeling to begin with. Not just the ones that occurred at Wolf's Run.* Rachel decided to sleep on it. If she felt the same way in the morning, she'd call Rose and tell her she needed a few more days.

CHAPTER 14

More of Rachel's Personal Bests –
Wednesday; November 11, 1964; 6:00 AM

R ose had been understanding as usual, when Rachel called to say she needed a few more days at Wolf's Run. As she hung up the phone, Rachel felt the first thrums of anticipation for what was to come. She'd led a colorful life, and couldn't wait to reminisce over its most tawdry details. Rachel believed the process of reliving past events would have the same restorative effect, whether they'd occurred at Wolf's Run or not. If so, in a way, today's musings would be groundbreaking, because she'd never tried it before.

After breakfast, Rachel merrily hit the trail with her packed lunch and water bottles. There, she immersed herself instantly into the time between Max's demise and high school graduation. She recalled feeling slighted, over her parents having such a hard time getting over the loss of Max. She used this feeling as motivation to excel at everything. She thought that by excelling, her parents would come to realize the exceptional nature of their surviving child, and eventually see the loss of Max as a bump on the road.

After high school, Rachel received a full-ride scholarship to Lawrence University, a well-regarded private liberal arts college in Appleton, WI. She majored in psychology and pulled straight-As while finishing her degree in three and a half years. Thereafter, she went off to Madison and earned her law degree at the University of Wisconsin. After passing the bar exam on her first try, she returned to the family home in Sheboygan, to work in the family business.

Although furious to find that her parents still hadn't gotten over the loss of Max, Rachel managed to hide it well. Over time, she began to sense that one or both of her parents harbored suspicions that she'd had a role in Max's unfortunate end. Rachel went to great lengths to discourage this line of thinking, but as time wore on the suspicions persisted, and her resentment grew.

Meanwhile, Ben's mentoring of his daughter continued, and was taken to a new level when he shared what might be considered the family's crown jewels. His ancestors passed down to Ben, summaries of every successful past family swindle. To these, he added summaries of his own. Once aware that these summaries existed, Rachel's thirst for the knowledge within them became unquenchable.

Rachel burned the midnight oil, studying these "family trophies". They enabled her to literally relive the thrills her ancestors had felt. The physical response they aroused … nape hairs standing, tingling, and so on … remarkably, was identical to what she'd felt sacrificing hatchlings and murdering Max. The elevated acuity these sensations brought, enabled her to grasp the various swindle styles instinctively. Better yet, even upon first reading, she'd been able to envision swindle variations that would've created greater windfall profits than the originals.

Rachel had already known she possessed an extraordinarily sharp legal mind, now she knew her illegal one was even better. She was organized, creative, resourceful, and had an exceptional ability to read people. Max's best had always been a distant second to hers. With all she had to offer, Rachel just couldn't understand why her parents continued to pine over Max. They needed to get over it, and if they didn't soon, Rachel feared she'd take matters into her own hands.

Then one day out of the blue, Ben confronted Rachel over whether she'd had a hand in Max's death. Always the superior liar, Rachel instantly snapped on an incredulous smile, and asked if he'd lost his mind. When Ben didn't back down, she feigned being offended, and firmly denied it. Then she gradually charmed him into seeing how ridiculous his suggestion had been. Ben's doubts subsided with the help of Rachel's thespian skills, and he soon apologized.

Ben hadn't realized it at the time, but he'd made a terrible mistake. From that day forward, Rachel viewed him more as a specimen to study and discard, than as a father. She continued to maintain the demeanor of a loving daughter, but her ambitions had changed. Previously, her ambition had been to take over the reins of the family business as soon as Ben was ready to give them up. Now, she planned to supplant Ben at the helm as quickly as possible.

The more Rachel studied the family trophies, the more her admiration for Ben faded. By Wolf family standards, Ben clearly hadn't been the sharpest tool in the shed. In fact, Ben's father Jacob hadn't been much better. With Jacob and Ben at the helm, the growth of legitimate businesses had been emphasized, swindling had been relegated to a sideline, and the Wolf name had been hidden from public view. She wasn't sure why, but all of this troubled Rachel deeply.

The family's current legitimate business was banking. Ben had managed to gain control of the Fond du Lac regional bank, after many years of wheeling and dealing, building off of Jacob's foundation. With nothing more to teach her in Sheboygan, Ben suggested Rachel relocate to Fond du Lac to learn the banking business. Bored, she jumped at the opportunity. Ben chaired the bank's board, and when the next vacancy came up, he manipulated the process in Rachel's favor. Once on the board, Rachel's performance quickly established her as heir apparent.

Keen to secure the family's next generation, Ben encouraged Rachel to take an interest in one of Fond du Lac's most eligible bachelors, Wes Barber, the bank's president. Rachel played along and to her delight, Wes did indeed turn out to be reliably-hard. However, her ulterior motive for the relationship had nothing to do with her father's line of thinking. Rachel wanted real-time access to all goings-on at the bank, and as bank president, she figured Wes was in a position to provide it. As time wore on, Rachel appreciated the real-time intel, but resented the expected quid pro quo. Always creative, Rachel soon came up with a scheme to keep Wes properly motivated, while relieving her of those unwanted duties.

Using her Madison contacts, Rachel hired a professional practitioner of buggery to make a house call. On the appointed night, she invited Wes to her apartment, something she'd done many times before. This time, however, she drugged Wes's cocktail. After letting him marinade for a while, she invited in her male mercenary wearing nothing but chaps. While the boys got acquainted, Rachel settled into a chair with her camera, to enjoy the show. A few snapshots of a naked Wes on his elbows and knees, being teased from behind by El Chapo, were all that were necessary. From that day forward, Rachel received the daily bank president's briefing, and any quid pro quo was only at Rachel's option and initiative.

Rachel was absolutely adamant that the family's next generation carry the surname Wolf. She discounted the idea of marrying Wes Barber, or any other man. Keeping her maiden-name, in those days, would draw too much attention. Besides, Rachel swung both ways, wanted all her diverse needs met on a regular basis, and a husband would only get in the way.

Rachel spent a fair amount of time trying to envision how she wanted her life to unfold. Some aspects were crystal-clear while others, such as how to have a child named Wolf, were less so. Crystal-clear, was her aspiration to be the family's greatest swindler of all time, no small feat in a bloodline of great swindlers. But she'd enough self-awareness to know this wouldn't leave time for motherhood, and in any event, she was poorly wired for the job. After some thought, she concluded getting pregnant would be easier than caring for the child. Inclined to solve the hardest problems first, she started looking for the right woman.

After shopping around, Rachel found the perfect little missy with all the maternal instincts one could possibly hope for. Rose was young, hot, and insatiable.

Better yet, she willingly signed a contract agreeing to serve as nanny for Rachel's future child. According to the agreement, Rose would move in when the baby came, and would serve as Rachel's nanny with benefits. Of course, Rachel retained the right to have her fun with anyone else she fancied, man or woman. In exchange, Rose received the joys of motherhood and the assurance she'd be *taken care of for life*. Apparently, Rose interpreted this clause to mean free room and board, a lifetime of luxury, and whatnot. Silly girl.

With child care arranged, Rachel turned her attention to having a baby. Although getting pregnant was easy enough, she also had to keep up appearances and protect her reputation. In a place like Fond du Lac, even a bigwig at the bank couldn't expect to have a baby out of wedlock and live happily ever after. People would talk and her parents wouldn't approve.

After more creative thought, Rachel came up with a socially acceptable scheme to end up with a baby but no man. She regularly shopped in Chicago, and used the opportunity of one of those trips to engage the services of an actor to play the role of her husband. On the same day, the actor recruited two members of his troupe to portray his parents. Once pregnant, she and the three actors would stage a whirlwind courtship and small family wedding. Afterward, she'd have the faux husband move into her Fond du Lac home for a month or so, and then be lost in a tragic accident while traveling on business. Soon after, Rachel would reveal the miracle of being pregnant, and swear to selflessly dedicate the rest of her life to raising the child sired by her one true love. After the child was born, even the townsfolk of Fond du Lac wouldn't begrudge her the help of a live-in nanny.

With the new hubby and in-laws under contract, rehearsing their parts and standing by, Rachel refocused on securing a sperm donor and getting pregnant. In her view, Wes wasn't bright enough, and even if he were, she preferred a stranger she'd never see again. *But who?* One Sunday afternoon Rachel poured a glass of wine, turned on the TV, and sat down to ponder that question. On came a football game, Packers versus Bears, and lightning struck. *Why not a Green Bay Packer?*

Back in her Lawrence University days, Rachel had spent a number of hormone-driven school breaks and weekends chasing Packers. St. Norbert College, where the Packers trained, was only a half-hour drive away. Another 15 minutes got you to Green Bay City Stadium, where the Packers played their games. The more Rachel thought about it, the more convinced she became that one of those bright, athletic hunks would make the perfect sperm donor. After all, they weren't exactly looking for a long-term relationship either.

Back in the day, Rachel had managed to nail a few practice-squad guys at St. Norbert, but never a real Packer. Drop-dead gorgeous co-eds like her were a dime a dozen, waiting outside the locker room door. The real Packers passed them over for more mature women, who were just as gorgeous but also sophisticated. Now 32 years old and in her prime, Rachel was confident she'd be exactly the kind of woman a real Packer would want nowadays.

While a co-ed, out of curiosity, Rachel had followed a few of those real-Packer instant couples, just to see where they went. The Union Hotel in De Pere was a popular destination. Under the soft lighting in the booth room, they'd have an intimate dinner in one of the two-seater booths, and then go upstairs to a room. Rachel decided she'd give it a try. After consulting her personal female calendar and the Packers home game schedule, she booked rooms at the Union Hotel for the night of every home game that overlapped ovulation. Pregnant two months into the season, Rachel canceled the rest of the bookings and pulled the trigger on her faux courtship and wedding. She told her soon-to-be husband to dye his hair golden blond, but she never said why.

When Rachel first broke the news of her engagement, Ben and Ruth were incredulous. Having anticipated the reaction, Rachel reminded her parents she'd always been decisive. To hear her tell it, it should've been no surprise to see her snap up her one-and-only soul mate, once he came along. The next weekend the lucky man and his parents visited the Wolf's and Rachel in Sheboygan. Any lingering disbelief on the part of Ben and Ruth, was dispelled instantly. As a tribute to the skill of these actors, the concocted backstories came across as the god's honest truth. Ruth was also taken by her future son-in-law's blond wavy hair.

The following weekend, a small family wedding was held at Ben and Ruth's mansion in Sheboygan. The happy couple decided to defer their honeymoon until the following summer, and the groom moved into Rachel's mansion in Fond du Lac. Rachel so enjoyed the charade, that a month later when hubby met his phony demise, she truly felt saddened. She drew upon and amplified this authentic feeling to portray herself as grief-stricken, and on the verge of total collapse.

After a respectful period, Rachel shared with Ben and Ruth the miraculous news of her pregnancy. Rachel's unusually rapid recovery from such a great loss had raised eyebrows with her parents, but a baby on the way made it seem more plausible. To bury their remaining suspicions, Rachel became outspoken about her plan to devote the remainder of her life to the unborn child. She vowed to remain faithful to her lost soulmate forever, and restored her maiden name. As the pregnancy progressed, Rachel made a big show of finding a nanny and, with the nanny's help, setting up the baby's room. And so it was, that Rachel's child would bear the surname Wolf.

Suddenly, the fading daylight caught Rachel's attention. Surprised, she checked her pack, only to find the lunch consumed and water bottles empty. Apparently, she'd been so absorbed in her own internal narrative, the entire day out on the trails had passed unnoticed. She looked at her watch, and shook her head in disbelief. Then, she stopped hiking to study her surroundings. Confident she knew her location, Rachel changed directions and headed back to the main house.

* * *

That night Rachel slept well, and by morning a little of her old swagger had returned. *Wolf's Run really did have restorative powers! Even when reliving memories from elsewhere!* Ecstatic, she couldn't wait to get back outside. She showered quickly, dressed for another day on the trails, and hurried to the kitchen. There, she wolfed down breakfast, told the housekeeper to surprise her with the evening cocktail selection and dinner menu, and was out the door. By the time Rachel rounded the out buildings, she was back in the flow state, picking up her memories where she'd left off the previous day.

Rachel's plan had been working to perfection until one day during her second trimester, when Ben casually remarked about her extraordinary bad luck with men, in reference to her husband and brother. Although left unsaid, Ben's tone insinuated he felt this coincidence to be highly unlikely. Rachel tried to deflect the moment with an incredulous smile, but when that didn't work, she flew into a rage. She demanded to know what possible motive she'd have to get rid of the father of her child. Ben had no ready answer, but he didn't back down. As she stomped off, Rachel told him he'd better apologize, or he'd never see his grandchild. Once out of sight, she allowed her feral smile to surface. Ben didn't know it yet, but he'd just sealed his own fate.

Rachel felt compelled to move quickly. Ben had become a chronic problem, and she needed to remove that cancer before it spread. She needed a plan, and set her laser-like mind to the task of developing one. Ironically, the pieces fell quickly into place, facilitated by Ben's own family business succession plan. He'd already begun to implement it, which made Rachel privy to certain important matters, such as her parent's wills and the details of their trusts. These insights plus calling in an old favor, were all she needed.

Ben had taken flying lessons at Chapman's Airpark east of Plymouth back in the late 1940s. Once licensed to fly he acquired a private plane, kept it at the airpark, and used an aviation services firm to maintain, fuel, and store it. Ben enjoyed flying the family on vacation jaunts here and there. These excursions brought Rachel to the airpark during her precocious early high school years, where one of the firm's mechanics took a shine to her. Flattered by the attentions of a full-grown man, Rachel began paying him more regular visits once licensed to drive. She fantasized about cockpit sex with oily callused hands all over her body, and he'd been more than happy to oblige. She soon tired of him, and threatened to break it off. But he pleaded with her, so she agreed to continue with the understanding that someday she'd need a big favor in return.

When Sheboygan County Memorial Airport opened in 1960, the aviation services firm moved its operations there, and Ben's plane followed. Over the years, Rachel managed to visit the airport often enough to keep her admiring mechanic interested. So it was, when in the spring of 1962, Rachel called in her chit in advance of the family's annual private flight to Louisville, for the Kentucky Derby. She provided a small device, and the mechanic spliced it into the plane's fuel line, no questions asked. The ingenious little contraption was designed to cause a fuel leak, ignite the fuel, and then melt in the fire and fall away. Rachel knew the flight plan by heart, and arranged for the maker to have the device automatically trigger when the plane reached cruising altitude. By then, the plane would be over the middle of Lake Michigan, south of Sheboygan.

The entire family always looked forward to the Kentucky Derby trip, but Rachel backed out unexpectedly at the last minute. Being pregnant and only a few months from full term, she felt it prudent to stay home. After seeing Ben and Ruth off, she returned to her Fond du Lac mansion. There, she created a script and rehearsed her lines, while waited for the evening TV news to come on. The lead story concerned a private plane that'd called in a mayday, given a position over Lake Michigan, and then gone silent. Search and rescue efforts were underway, but names were being withheld pending notification of next of kin.

After the news broke, Rachel conjured severe distress and called the Louisville hotel, to ask whether her parents had checked in. They hadn't, of course, so she worked herself into full-blown hysteria. Then, she placed a call to the authorities and replicated the performance, sobbing uncontrollably all the while. Within the hour, the authorities arrived to take her statement, and promised she'd be the first to know when anything further was learned.

After a few days, Ben and Ruth were presumed dead and the search refocused on recovery. After a week, the authorities assumed Ben must've called in the wrong coordinates in his panic, so they widened the search area. It wasn't until a month later, that the wreckage and bodies were found in 490 feet of water. Given the state of Ben's body, the autopsy couldn't rule out an acute medical issue such as stroke or heart attack. Everything about the plane had been damaged, but the investigation couldn't rule out that the damage was simply a result of the crash. When all was said and done, the crash was ruled accidental.

Rachel spent the month of the search cloistered at home with Ruth, presumably grief-stricken at the loss of her parents and unable to face the public. Whenever the authorities checked in with their latest update, she played her part to perfection. Once the crash was ruled accidental, the structure of the trusts bypassed probate and made Rachel sole heir immediately. Rachel became the controlling owner of Fond du Lac regional bank, and assumed her late father's role as chair of the board of directors. In hindsight, Rachel knew she never could've concocted such a perfect scheme, without being privy to the wills and trusts of her parents. These told her

Ruth had to go, too. In a sense, Ruth had been collateral damage.

* * *

That evening after dinner, Rachel took to the trails once more, to hike to the overlook of the Menominee River rapids. She felt rejuvenated but wanted to test the level of her recovery, and knew exactly how to do it. After building a bonfire in the fire pit, she settled onto a bed of pine needles and leaned back against a smooth and comfy boulder.

Before long, Rachel lost herself in the ambiance of the fire and the wildness of the scene. It was as if she'd simply relaxed and become a part of it. The tree canopy above, highlighted by the glow of the fire, swayed noticeably in the stiff breeze. The various trees appeared out of synch, their branches alternately slapping each other, then opening wide vistas to the starry sky above. The motion caused smoke to swirl as if captured, then billow toward an upward escape. Undulating, the branches appeared two-toned, with undersides warmly lit by the fire in stark contrast to the cold light of the moon, falling from above. Firelight danced among the randomly strewn surfaces of boulders, tree trunks, and under growth. Here and there, from deep in the forest, glowing eyes reminded Rachel that she wasn't alone. Instead, she was a part of something much larger.

Focusing now on sound, Rachel could hear the crackling of the fire, the creak and groan of the trees, and the brushing together of the branches. The river's falls contributed the timbre of rushing water, direct and echoed. From nearby on the left came the *who-*

cooks-for-you of a Barred Owl, and far off to the right, the whinnying of a Screech-Owl. Yips from a group of coyotes came from beyond the river. But under it all, and much closer, was something else. Breathing, perhaps. No, panicked breathing, then a snort and the rustle of a deer taking flight. Instantly, wolf howls exploded from everywhere.

Rachel leapt from her resting place, and positioned herself to the upwind side of the fire. From there, she peered outward, into the darkness. The smell of fear was everywhere, overlayed with the scent of hunger about to be satisfied. Life or death, each hurtling through the underbrush this way and that, like vectors of sound. As the cocktail of adrenalin and dopamine coursed through her body, Rachel radiated a sense of feral invincibility. She slowly spun a 360, marveling as she went, at her own elevated acuities of smell, hearing, and sight. Deep inside a thrum began to build. Her nape-hairs stood on end. Tingling enveloped her breasts and groin, shot down her limbs, and exploded into her fingers and toes. She bent deeply to exhale, reloaded her lungs as she shot back to attention, and let out an apex predator roar. She held the blood-curdling note for an eternity ... hands bawled into fists, neck veins and tendons bulging, and mouth and eyes wide open. When the moment passed there was no doubt ... Rachel was back to her old self.

CHAPTER 15

The Old Rachel Returns – Friday; November 13, 1964; 12:00 Noon

Back to her old self, Rachel returned to Fond du Lac, arriving about noon. After a sweet homecoming with Rose and Jake over lunch, she went to the study and called Vince. Darkwater Flint had yet to be found, so she told Vince to keep looking and try harder. But the Evans news was intriguing. James and Mary Evans had joined the Sheboygan County chapter of something called the NFO. She instructed Vince to infiltrate the chapter, and find out what that's all about.

After a few days of quality time with Rose and Jake, Rachel drove to Madison. There, she researched the NFO using the various libraries of the University of Wisconsin. In the general library, she ran down recent media mentions of the organization in the nation's major newspapers, farm magazines, and whatnot. From there, she went to the ag library, to gain a full understanding of the NFO's mission, strategy, major actions since being founded in 1955, and outcomes achieved thus far. There'd been mention of litigation, so she went to the law library to research the cases. By the end of November, Rachel was back in Fond du Lac, and one of the nation's leading experts on the NFO.

Meanwhile, Vince paid a visit to his big brother 'Milwaukee Phil', to find a mob thug that looked more like a farmer than a goombah. Once one was found, Vince took him shopping to acquire dairy farmer attire, which they washed and dried five times to achieve a well-worn appearance. After some crash-course tutoring, on the evening of December 1st, Vince sent him to the Sheboygan County NFO chapter meeting with instructions to keep his mouth shut, listen, and report back. On a call to Rachel late that night, Vince told her the chapter was considering various market interventions to jack up the price for raw milk, but hadn't settled on one yet.

By the end of the following day, Rachel had concocted the outline of a swindle. Her concept was to make the swindle look exactly like an NFO market intervention. She'd make the faux intervention so appealing, the NFO chapter would surely adopt it. Once that happened ... well ... good things would fall her way ... things that should've fallen already. But the plan was complex, and she needed help to pull it off. Vince's brother, Phil, was a likely source for the kind of help she needed. To bring in Phil, she knew there'd need to be something appealing in it for him and his masters. Rather than guess what that might be, she had Vince set up a call so she could ask him.

After exchanging pleasantries, Rachel explained her idea, and then said, "Phil, to do this I'll need your help. I can structure it so both of us see harvestable opportunities. That way, no money need change hands, so there'll be less risk. I know what I want out of the deal, but not what might appeal to you. If you can give me an idea, I'll update the plan and we'll talk again soon."

After a moment of empty air, Phil admitted, "You know, I think I do see a couple of things here. We've had our eyes on the Wisconsin dairy industry for a very long time. It's so squeaky-clean, it makes me puke. Down in the Chicago area, we're sort of in the transportation business, if you know what I mean, and that includes milk transportation. We've a nice little understanding with all the dairies. Our guys haul all the milk and we get our slice … or else. It's worked out very nicely for everybody … sort of a win-win. In our view, it's silly to have all these little dairies up here in Wisconsin, packaging beverage milk for the few hayseeds that live here. National supermarket chains are the wave of the future. They want to sell store-brand milk, and only the big Chicago-area dairies have the capacity to handle accounts like that."

Rachel's eyes narrowed, "Let me rephrase that in my own words. Then, you tell me if I've got it right. In your view, diverting Wisconsin Grade A raw milk to the Chicago area would be an opportunity, because then you could haul it."

Phil nodded, "That's exactly right … and oh, by the way. We'd also haul the packaged beverage milk back up to the supermarkets in Wisconsin. We'd kind of get them coming and going, if you know what I mean."

Rachel's eyebrows went up, "Huh … well, that is interesting. So, do you see any other opportunities?"

Phil took a moment, then said wisely, "As a matter of fact, I do. This NFO outfit has been popping up all over, you know, and it concerns us. Supermarkets experiment with milk pricing, and when prices go up people buy less. If the supermarkets are going to keep consumer prices low, we can't have the NFO stirring up shit among the farmers, and jacking up the price of raw milk. This is America for crumb-sake, if farmers want to earn more money, they should work harder … or whatever. That NFO needs to be put in its place. Otherwise, sooner or later, what they're doing will put pressure on our slice of the pie."

Rachel stifled a giggle, and said, "Well, trust me, the plan I've got in mind will be the NFO's rudest awakening ever." She thought a moment, then lowered her voice, "But I haven't worked out all the details yet. Can you think of anything you already have going on, that might serve as a building block?"

Phil pondered this, "Well, we've got a licensed cheese maker in our hip pocket, if that helps. As fate would have it, his teenage daughter ran away, and became employed at one of our titty bars here in Milwaukee. Then somehow, she got hooked on the needle. That's an expensive habit, so the enterprising gal's been providing extra benefits to patrons on the side, if you know what I mean. We make more on the side business, so it's another win-win. Anyway, we've promised to bring an opportunity to this cheese maker, and if he does well with it, we'll detox his daughter and send her home. With his credentials, we figured he might be able to help us break into the Wisconsin cheese business. But cheese seems to be a tough nut to crack, and we haven't found anything yet."

Rachel chewed on her lower lip, then said thoughtfully, "Okay, let me think about that. Maybe in a day or two, I'll be ready for another call."

Phil exhaled heavily, and said, "You do that. And Rachel, thanks for thinking of us. Always a pleasure doing business with you." Then he raised his voice, "Say Vince, you still there, or have you fallen asleep?"

Vince laughed, "I'm still here big brother."

In a boisterous voice, Phil said, "You need to come down and visit again. We could maybe introduce you to the cheese maker's daughter ..."

* * *

The next day, Vince set up a second call. After the small talk, Rachel explained her scheme in far greater detail than before. It had a lot of moving parts, with the cheese maker serving as a major cog.

When she finished, Phil said, "Give me a minute to roll that around in my mind." He hummed a few bars of the Drifters' *'Under the Boardwalk'*, and when ready said, "So, let me get this straight. You'll find a choice cheese factory for us to scarf up, using our cheese maker as a front. To make sure the investment is safe and never traceable to us, we'll title the physical assets under the name of the cheesemaker's wife. When the scam is over and things have cooled down, she'll resell the cheese factory. If she wants her family to live, she'll sign the money back over to us, and we get our investment back. That's the first part, right?"

Rachel, with an encouraging lilt in her voice, "Yes, exactly. Keep going, I think you've got it."

More confident now, Phil continued, "Okay, so we set up a phony LLC, and use that to sign a contract with the Sheboygan County NFO. Under the contract, the NFO diverts their member's milk to our plant, while they're trying to negotiate a higher milk price with their current processor. Of course, we never have any intention of paying for their milk, or making cheese with it. Instead, they haul it to us each day, and we turn around and haul it to wherever we want each night. Rachel, am I still on the right-track?"

Rachel laughed, "You're killing it. Keep going."

Delighted, Phil soldiered on, "Okay, now it'd be reasonable to presume that the NFO and its farmers might get a little testy, and come after our investment. So, to protect ourselves we make sure there's no recourse under the contract except against the assets of the LLC, which of course are zero. But since some judges might allow another avenue of recourse against the officers of the LLC, we make sure the cheese maker is the only officer named … and oh by the way, he's penniless, too … since, you know, everything's in his wife's name. So, try as they may, we keep our investment plus get their milk for a period of time." He thought for a moment, then said, "Huh … any idea how long we'd be able to drag out these shenanigans? The longer the better, right?"

Rachel, with a new friskiness in her voice, "Well, this is the fun part, but it's also a little tricky. During negotiations, it's important that the current processor doesn't cave in to the NFO. If that happens, the diversion ends. To keep holding out, the current processor will need an alternate source of milk … meaning …"

As Rachel went silent, her thinking slowly dawned on Phil, "Oh my god! Rachel, you've got to be shitting me! I love it!"

Rachel laughed again, "I thought you might. So, if you become the alternate supplier, they'd be able to hold out indefinitely. Then the shenanigans can last until the farmers realize they've been screwed. Pay them monthly, and it'll be at least a month and a week before the checks start bouncing. If you've got a good story for when they come calling, maybe you can string them along for another month or so. By then, the farmers will all be desperate, and ready to lynch the NFO. If you play your cards right, maybe they'll sign with you to haul their milk permanently. An aspirational goal might be to sign more-and-more farmers, until you've cornered enough milk to start gobbling up Wisconsin dairies. The sky's the limit."

Phil snorted a feral-edged laugh, "I love the way you think, Rachel. I've got to hand it to you, this's exactly what we've been looking for." He paused a moment to reflect, "I'm tempted to agree verbally on the spot, but the investment is not insignificant. Just to be safe, I'm going to run this past my masters in Chicago. I don't anticipate a problem but … you know … the higher ups are sometimes aware of things I'm not. I'll get back to you." Within an hour, the mob was in.

* * *

The next day, Saturday December 4th, Rachel rolled up her sleeves and started pulling strings. One of her favorites was a staffer she had dirt on, at the banking division of the Wisconsin Department of Financial Institutions. He'd been convicted of bank fraud in Pennsylvania, and relocated to Wisconsin to start over. As fate would have it, a friend of Rachel's from law school was practicing in Pennsylvania, and handled the case. Several years ago, Rachel ran into this friend at an airport bar. Lawyers often share war stories, within the discretionary limits of the law of course, but after a few drinks her friend became a little loose-lipped. Rachel recognized the felon's name as soon as she said it, because she had dealings at Wisconsin's banking division, and he now worked there.

Since then, this poor bastard has been at Rachel's beck and call. Her Saturday morning Jing-a-ling went straight to his home. When he picked up on the second ring, she said in a so-glad tone, "Well hello there, it's me again. Tomorrow, I need another care package by courier. Inside will be the contact information for every dairy farmer currently indebted to Oostburg Bank, and the date when Oostburg pays their next quarterly-dividend."

His wife was home, so in a whisper the staffer said, "Oh come on, Rachel! Disclosing the names of a bank's debtors is a Class 1 felony, I can't do that!"

Rachel dropped her voice, "You can, and you will … or else. Besides, I've made it easy for you, the office will be empty on Saturday." Then, she clicked off.

One whole wall of Rachel's study was clad in cork board. She spent the rest of Saturday acquiring the most detailed map of Sheboygan County currently available in print, and mounting it on the cork board. The map had been developed by the Post Office and showed every road, including those surfaced with gravel or dirt, and ones used only for logging. Most importantly, every current RFD mail delivery route was traced. On Sunday, after the courier package arrived, Rachel used the map to pin the locations of every dairy farmer indebted to Oostburg Bank. Most to least, these farmers were spread across the townships of Holland, Lima, Sherman, Wilson, Lyndon, Scott, and Mitchell.

Next, Rachel pulled the latest Wisconsin Cheese Makers Association membership directory out of her bookshelf. Onto a pad of paper, she transcribed the name, address, and phone number of every cheese factory in the seven-township area, as well as the names and phone numbers of the licensed cheese makers serving each plant. Then, she meticulously pinned onto the map, the locations of each cheese factory. She used the scale of the map to roughly estimate distances, and concluded that any of these cheese factories would be within reasonable hauling distance from every farmer pinned.

Rachel spent the rest of Sunday on a field trip. First, she drove past each cheese factory, to gain a comparative sense of them. Then, she narrowed in on several factories that appeared under-utilized or closed. To learn why, she made discreet inquiries at nearby gas stations, country stores, or villages. Particularly intriguing, was an idled plant in the Town of Mitchell. It's owner, a cheese maker that'd nearly died from a recent heart attack, had been forced to shut down. Although seeking a buyer, he hadn't found one yet. This plant's refrigerated bulk-milk storage towers and cheesemaking facilities were among the largest she'd seen. In other words, it's perfect.

That evening, Rachel got caught up on the news and sports, while Rose cleaned up the dinner dishes and readied Jake for bed. Feeling a little guilty, she volunteered to put Jake down to sleep when the time came. After he dozed off, Rachel stood there admiring her little man for a moment. Then, she gently patted his golden blond mop top, and cooed, "Rosie tells me the two of you watched the Packers game today. Did you see daddy? He helped beat those big bad Bears, didn't he? Scored a touchdown and kicked a field goal." Watching the game with her son could've been a special moment. Rachel wondered how many she had missed by being so overly focused on work.

First thing Monday, Rachel and Phil spoke again.

She shared the details on the cheese factory, and then they talked timing. Rachel emphasized, "Every aspect of the swindle lines up perfectly, end-to-end, if you have possession of that plant by the end of December."

Now serious, Phil dropped his voice, "That's not a problem, Rachel. I'll throw enough money around to make that happen."

* * *

Rachel spent the rest of Monday working out how to draw in and persuade Oostburg Bank's farmers to voluntarily divert their milk to Phil's plant. As a scholar of the NFO and its programs, Rachel knew of a pilot program being tested in Iowa and Missouri called *Roaming Reps*. The concept was to recruit retired farmers that're true believers in the NFO cause, and have them assist county chapters that're just getting started, or trying to mount new programs. Rachel had burned a copy of the *Roaming Reps Pilot Program Training Manual* while at the ag library, and found it to be a fascinating read. She'd also read an article in one of the farm magazines, claiming early successes in the pilots.

For Rachel to use *Roaming Reps* in her scheme, the local chapter couldn't know it wasn't yet available in Wisconsin. She knew the NFO wouldn't promote the program through official channels until after the pilots were completed, and deemed successful. But it's possible a chapter member might've heard about the pilots, and knew the program wasn't yet launched nationwide. By attending the NFO's national convention, for instance, or by reading the same magazine she had. Curious now, she had Vince find out from his spy whether the term had been mentioned at the last chapter meeting. Roaming reps hadn't been mentioned.

Rachel decided to take the calculated risk, and make *Roaming Reps* an integral part of her plan. She reasoned that if a rep showed up at the doorstep of the chapter president, he'd be thrilled to have the pro bono help. Since the chapter was recently formed and all the members were new to the NFO, she doubted any of them were aware of the program. Mind made up, she felt a thrum of adrenalin, as another piece fell into place.

Rachel's next challenge was to find someone to pose as the NFO roaming rep. To pull off a stunt like that, she needed somebody that'd been a real dairy farmer sometime during his adult life. Out of necessity, this person would be privy to part of the swindle, which meant absolute leverage over him was required. After mulling that over, she realized any dairy farmer behind on his loan with one of her branch banks would be a good prospect. The next morning Rachel called Wes, and told him she wanted files on all such dairy farmers on her desk by close-of-business, or COB, Friday. Over the weekend, Rachel studied the files and made a short list of candidates.

First thing Monday morning, Rachel began calling the cognizant farm loan officers at her branch banks for additional information on her candidates. By early afternoon, her interest was piqued by Bert and Ernie Baker, brothers running a dairy farm near Campbellsport, in Fond du Lac County. They'd been in default for over a year on a loan with her Campbellsport branch, and the regional bank's legal department was already gearing up to officially takeover the farm.

Ernie was in his late 50s, never worked outside the

farm, and would likely have trouble finding a job if they lost it. Bert was old enough to retire but hadn't paid into Social Security, so if he did, there'd be nothing for him to live on. In other words, both desperately needed to hang onto the farm. Another interesting tidbit, Bert's been selling seed corn on side, and doing pretty well at it. In other words, Bert had a sales personality.

Mid-afternoon, Rachel called back the farm loan officer handling the Baker brothers, and told him to set up a private meeting for her with them at the branch bank ASAP. Later that day, he called back to say the meeting was set for first thing the following morning. At the meeting, Rachel offered to write off half the Baker's debt and postpone liquidation of their farm for one year, if they did exactly what she said and kept their mouths shut. If the outcome turned out as hoped, after the year was up, she promised to restructure their remaining debt so the farm operation and seed corn sales could service it, while providing them a modest living.

In exchange for the sweetheart deal, Bert would have to assume another name, Al Stone, and pose as an NFO roaming rep assigned to assist the Sheboygan County chapter. In that capacity, he'd recruit new chapter members from a list of dairy farmers provided by Rachel. Then, he'd steer the chapter president to promote among his members, the concept of diverting their milk to a specific cheese factory, while the NFO tried to negotiate a higher milk price with the original processor. Ernie would play himself, but serve as a phony reference for his brother. When the Sheboygan County chapter president called to check up on Al Stone, Ernie would sing his praises. The backstory would be that Ernie was in the midst of organizing an NFO chapter in Fond du Lac

County, and Al's help had been a godsend. When Rachel finished explaining the deal, Bert and Ernie looked at each other, shrugged, and signed on.

CHAPTER 16

Rachel Puts Her Plan in Play – Monday;
December 14, 1964; 9:00 AM

After successfully recruiting Bert and Ernie to her cause, Rachel spent the next week mentoring her new charges. She left a pile of NFO propaganda with the Baker brothers, and visited them regularly. When she felt he was ready, Rachel suggested that Bert (aka Al Stone) call the Sheboygan County NFO chapter president, Abe Van Driest. She tutored him on what to say, to gain Van Driest's trust. She also made sure Bernie knew exactly what to say as All Stone's reference, when Van Driest called.

Rachel's first adrenalin rush came when word returned that Van Driest had invited Stone to the January 5th NFO chapter meeting. The game was on. Under Rachel's tutelage, Stone mostly listened at the meeting, got to know people, and received Van Driest's blessing to assist with recruiting new members. Rachel gave Stone the list of dairy farmers to target, and told him to get cracking.

Meanwhile, Rachel kept in close communication

with Phil. As promised, Phil had taken possession of the Town of Mitchell cheese factory in late December. Papini Cheese LLC was officially open for business, and Vito Papini and family had moved into the house on the premises.

After a week on the membership recruiting trail, Stone sensed he'd exceeded expectations. At Rachel's suggestion, he called Van Driest to schmooze and hopefully ingratiate himself further. New members had already begun rolling in, and Stone could tell Van Driest was hooked. While the iron was still hot, Rachel had Stone call Van Driest again, a few days later, and plant the seed that a cheese factory had just opened in Mitchell, and was hungry for milk.

The very next day, Van Driest called Stone to invite him along to a meeting he'd set up with Vito Papini for the following morning. Stone agreed, of course, and afterward called Rachel for advice. She coached him up, and he didn't let her down. At a critical juncture, Stone pulled Van Driest aside and gave him a hard sell on how this was the perfect opportunity they'd been looking for. Van Driest bit, and even deputized Stone to negotiate with Papini on his behalf, and secure an agreement in time to be voted forward at the February 2nd chapter meeting.

Rachel advised Stone to call Van Driest often during negotiations, and make him feel integrally involved. In particular, she knew NFO-central was currently promoting free bulk-milk hauling to aid chapters in their market interventions. She told Stone to ask Van Driest, as the county NFO chapter president, to call the national organization and officially place the request. He did, and the NFO agreed.

Behind the scenes, Rachel drafted the agreement and Phil reviewed it. By delegating the negotiation to Stone, Van Driest telegraphed that he wasn't a details man. This told Rachel he'd be unlikely to read it and raise questions. But just to be safe, she told Stone to tell Van Driest not to worry about the language, because it's based on the NFO's standard terms and conditions. In reality, of course, the agreement was custom-designed to garner the chapter's approval, while also making sure Phil got his money back plus a bunch of free milk.

Stone's gaslighting of Van Driest on the terms was masterful. Appealing to his ego, Stone laid it on thick about how essential it'd been, for Van Driest to secure NFO-central's commitment to haul milk for free. That, plus Papini's willingness to pay a premium over what cheese makers normally paid for milk, made all the difference. Chapter members would receive the same net price for their raw milk during the diversion to Papini, as they currently received from Verifine. Of course, they'd approve the deal.

According to the agreement, farmers would be paid monthly, and the milk diversion would begin March 1st. This date was selected for two reasons. First, Oostburg Bank pays a quarterly dividend at the end of February, so their retained earnings would be depleted then. Like many small banks in the area, Oostburg was on the *dairy farmer fiscal year*: Dec-Feb (doldrums), Mar-May (spring's work), Jun-Aug (peak milk), and Sep-Nov (harvest). Second, dairy farmers would've drawn their spring's work seasonal financing by then, putting them deeply in debt.

Always thinking ahead, Rachel worried that a farmer might ask ... *why March 1st* ... at the February

NFO meeting. Obviously, neither of the real reasons could be given, if this were to occur. Stumped on what a good answer might be, Rachel asked Stone, "So Al, I mean Bert, sorry. What's your answer if a farmer asks ... *why March 1st* ... at the NFO meeting. You can't very well tell the truth."

Bert thought for a moment, then said, "Milk supplies are at their leanest then, with many cows dried up in advance of the spring calving season. It's the perfect time to divert milk, because it'll be tough for Verifine to replace it."

Impressed, Rachel nodded, "Huh. Well, there you go. Say that."

Although Bert had played his role to perfection, Rachel knew the longer the game went on, the greater the chance he'd slip up. With that in mind, she decided to pull him out if the diversion was approved on February 2nd. The exit plan was simple. After the positive vote, Stone would attribute it to Van Driest's great leadership, and claim the NFO had reassigned him to help a less-capable chapter.

❋ ❋ ❋

The chapter voted to move forward with the diversion. With Stone's job done, the success of Rachel's plan now rested on Phil and his minions. On March 1st, the NFO hauled the milk of farmers participating in the diversion to Papini's plant. On the same day, Phil's ABC Milk Haulers LLC made an unsolicited sales call at Verifine in Sheboygan. When Verifine's president, Marty De Schmitt, was asked if he'd be interested in buying Chicago-area spot market milk, he nearly shit-his-pants in his haste to sign on. Via ABC, the diverted milk ended up at Verifine.

When Papini's end-of-month checks bounced, Rachel and Phil knew the NFO would come calling. To prepare Papini to string the NFO along, they crafted his story and coached his response. They'd hoped for another week to elapse before word got out on the bad checks, but instead they got two. At their urging, Papini initially dodged calls and visits, which bought Phil another week of free milk. By the time a fellow from the NFO's national organization arrived with a delegation of chapter locals, Papini had rehearsed his story to perfection. The clowns bought it, and agreed to continue to send their milk.

The NFO chapter met the first Wednesday of every month, placing the next meeting the night of May 4th. Although Papini's second checks would also bounce, at the meeting this wouldn't yet be known. Even so, at Rachel's urging, Phil decided to shutter the Papini plant and bail out after hauling away Wednesday's milk. He'd had a good run of free milk, and taking undue risks wasn't prudent.

From that point forward, Rachel and Phil worked independently to implement their separate parts of the remaining plan. In Rachel's view, they'd won the war and each had their own plunder to gather. She knew exactly what she needed to do, and her success no longer depended on Phil's. Although curious about how Phil intended to remain the milk hauler for those farmers, corner more milk over time, and so on … it really wasn't any of Rachel's business. Likewise, what Rachel was about to do, was no business of the mob's.

* * *

Driven by the thrill of the hunt, Rachel entered the end game. She called her favorite staffer at the banking division once more, and put in another urgent request. A courier-package arrived the following day, with the names and contact information for every shareholder of Oostburg Bank.

Rachel had already crafted her letter to the shareholders, but she'd been caught off guard by the sheer number of them. She didn't yet know when her missive needed to reach them, but when the time came, it had to happen pronto. The unforeseen production problem caused her to consider use of her regional bank. They'd plenty of capacity for such things, of course, but crossing that bright line between her legitimate and illegitimate businesses came with some risk.

Feeling the urgency, and unable to come up with a better idea, Rachel drove to the bank and pulled Wes out of a meeting. After being filled in with only what he needed to know, Wes took the letter and shareholder addresses, and spun-up the administrative staff. Several hours later, Rachel left the bank with boxes of completed packages, ready to be hand-carried to each shareholder when the time came. The letters, typed on blank stationary and left unsigned, ended with ... *Best Regards, Wealthy and Watching.* The sender information was left blank.

With all these pieces in place, Rachel's final step was to craft and submit by courier, an anonymous complaint to the Wisconsin Department of Financial Institutions. Once that was out of the way, Rachel poured a glass of wine, and was about to kick back when the phone rang.

Vince, hyped, "You're not going to believe this. We found Flint!"

Startled, Rachel jerked half upright and spilt her wine, "W-what?"

Vince laughed, "You heard me. We found Darkwater Flint!"

After a wicked giggle, Rachel said, "Give me a sec …" She went bottoms up, hurled the wine glass into the fireplace, and gushed, "Vince, that's the cherry on top of an already perfect day. Listen … call Phil … ask him to keep his best doer on standby. I've stirred up a shit storm, and I want Flint put down the same day it hits. Until then, keep him shadowed. It won't be long now."

CHAPTER 17

The Evans's Bet on the NFO – Wednesday;
February 2, 1965; 9:00 PM

T he president of the Sheboygan County NFO chapter, Abe Van Driest, communicated with members through a chain call, where he'd telephone a handful of members, they'd call others assigned to them, and so on. The previous day's message had been ... an exciting proposal to raise the price of milk will be voted on tomorrow night, so please be sure to attend.

Overdrive and Mary enjoyed an animated conversation on the way to the meeting, both feeling the thrum of anticipation. If the buzz in the meeting room was any indication, they weren't the only ones. Looking around, they'd been shocked at the size of the crowd. Soon, Van Driest called the meeting to order, and explained why the crowd was so large. To hear him tell it, Al Stone had single-handedly recruited enough new members to fill the room. Last month, Van Driest had introduced Stone as an NFO roaming rep assigned to their chapter to help them get things done. At the time, Stone had struck Overdrive as a slick sonofabitch, the kind of salesy type that made his skin crawl.

Van Driest asked each new member to stand and introduce themselves. Overdrive and Mary knew a few of these farmers, the names of others rang a bell, and the rest were total strangers. From the names, Overdrive guessed most were from Holland, Wilson, and Lima townships.

After the introductions, Van Driest launched into an explanation of the proposal to be voted on. As attendees already knew, they'd authorized the NFO to negotiate on their behalf with milk processors, as a condition of their membership. Verifine Dairy in Sheboygan, currently served as the beverage milk processor for most of them. The proposal was to divert member's milk elsewhere, temporarily, while NFO-central hammered out a new contract with Verifine. If all went well, farmers would return to Verifine after a short period, and thereafter receive higher prices for their Grade A raw milk under the new contract.

In structuring the proposal, the largest challenge had been finding a temporary buyer for the diverted milk. Fortunately, a cheese factory in the Town of Mitchell had recently reopened, and it had ample refrigerated milk storage and cheesemaking facilities to handle the volume. The new owner, Papini Cheese LLC, had already agreed to pay a premium over the typical raw milk price for cheesemaking, in order to jumpstart their business. In addition, as a show of support for the chapter, NFO-central had already agreed to haul milk to the Papini plant at no cost to participating farmers. Between the premium and free-hauling, participating farmers would be paid the same net price for milk during the diversion, as currently received from Verifine.

At this juncture, the room exploded with questions. A skeptical dutchman from the Town of Holland asked, "Have you done a background check on Papini?"

Van Driest shrugged, "Well, I wouldn't call it an official background check, but I've verified that he's a licensed cheese maker in the State of Wisconsin."

Again, the persistent dutchmen, "Never heard of him. Where's he from?"

Van Driest struggled to stifle a grin, "He made cheese in Kenosha County."

A voice of scorn from the back of the room, "Kenosha! Since when do they make cheese in Kenosha? I thought they just sold it at roadside stands, you know, to flatlanders crossing from Illinois." The room broke out in titters.

Van Driest held up his hands to quiet the crowd, and said a trifle impatiently, "Well, apparently they make a little cheese down there, too."

Not yet satisfied, Overdrive asked, "How'd you run across Papini?"

Van Driest pointed his thumb, "Al here stumbled onto them while beating the bushes for new members." Stone nodded and smiled.

Mary asked, "Is there a signed contract with Papini, or is this just verbal?"

Van Driest said wisely, "We've a signed contract, but it's only valid if the membership here votes to move forward with the milk diversion."

A farmer from the Town of Wilson shouted out, "Have you had a lawyer review it?" Overdrive and Mary's eyes met, and Mary mouthed *good question*.

Van Driest bobbed his head, "Well, it's probably even

better than that. The agreement is based on the NFO's standard contract, and Al says they've got a whole bevy of lawyers." Van Driest looked over at him, and Stone winked.

A farmer from the Town of Lima asked, "When would the diversion start?"

Van Driest nodded, now grim, "That's a really good question. The whole point of the diversion is to give the NFO maximum leverage in negotiations with Verifine. We've targeted March 1st, because the raw milk supply is leanest right around then. You know, because a lot of cows are dried up in advance of the spring calving season."

A scruffy-looking farmer from the Town of Scott asked, "How often does Papini pay us?"

Van Driest eyed the room, "By the first business day of each month, you'll have Papini's check in hand for the previous month's milk."

It went on like this for another half hour, and then Van Driest called for a vote. The membership voted unanimously to move forward. Only farmers currently sending their milk to Verifine could participate in the diversion, but even so, that was 36 dairy farmers.

At the end of the meeting, Stone got up and said, "I'd like to congratulate your Sheboygan County NFO Chapter President, Abe Van Driest, on his outstanding leadership. Without him, none of this would've happened." The room gave Van Driest an enthusiastic round of applause. Then, Stone said, "My work here's done, and the NFO has me moving on to another assignment. It's been a pleasure working with each and every one of you, and when you achieve a bump-up in milk prices, I can't wait to hear how big." The room exploded in cheers, then morphed into a standing ovation.

* * *

March 1st was on a Tuesday, so Monday afternoon the leader of NFO's negotiating team called Verifine's president, Marty De Schmitt, to say that starting tomorrow, three dozen of his suppliers would be sending their milk elsewhere. The NFO guy offered to visit De Schmitt that afternoon, and give him a list of farmers. That way, Verifine could avoid the expense of its haulers driving all over kingdom come for nothing the next day. De Schmitt saw the value in that, and when they met, agreed to schedule the first negotiating session for the following morning.

Starting Tuesday, NFO bulk-milk trucks made their rounds to the 36 farmers. It took a few days to optimize the routes, but thereafter deliveries to the Papini plant went smoothly. As promised, every farmer received their first Papini check on the first business day of April, which ironically happened to be April fool's day. Busy with spring's work, most farmers didn't immediately endorse their checks and mail them to the bank. Add in the snail's pace of RFD mail, plus banking system processing time, and two weeks passed before it became widely known that Papini's checks were bad.

Papini wouldn't return calls, so Van Driest reached out to NFO-central in a panic. They assigned an experienced market intervention trouble shooter, Otto Schwartz, to the case. Schwartz immediately called the NFO's lead negotiator with Verifine, for an update. Negotiations had progressed well, but both sides had played hard ball, and tensions ran high. The negotiator fretted that if word got out about Papini being insolvent, they'd lose all their leverage. Verifine would know that without Papini, the farmers had no staying power.

Schwartz hustled to Sheboygan County, but by the time a face meeting with Papini was set, another week had passed. Schwartz led a delegation to the meeting that included Van Driest and Overdrive and Mary, as the owners of the largest participating dairy farm. Papini was contrite, and claimed his original financier had let him down, so he'd changed to another. He admitted the old checks were bad, but claimed the new ones were good as gold. They'd arrive on schedule the following week, and be made out for both month's milk, to catch everybody up. To hear him tell it, the financing problem came out of the blue. He apologized profusely for any inconvenience this'd caused, and assured them all was good now. He claimed the money to back the new checks was already in his accounts.

* * *

On the way back from the Papini meeting, the group stopped at Phrang's in Cascade for lunch. Schwartz asked the others, "Well, what do you think?"

Overdrive and Mary deferred to Van Driest, "I don't know what to think."

Overdrive didn't hold back, "Papini is slick as shit."

Mary frowned, and said, "I'd like to stay optimistic, but I've a bad feeling."

Schwartz bobbed his head, "Me too. But the second checks are only about a week off, so we'll know for sure soon enough. For now, we might as well stay the course. Look, the NFO needs me to put out another fire in

Minnesota, so that's where I'll be in the meantime."

Van Driest nearly gagged, "You'll be back for our May 4th meeting, right?"

Schwartz nodded, "Wouldn't miss it for the world. It's just getting interesting around here."

Over the rest of lunch, Schwartz filled them in on how the negotiations with Verifine were going. If the second Papini checks were good, he predicted Verifine would cave and take all the farmers back at a higher milk price. If not, the NFO would cave, and pray everybody'd be taken back at the old price. Schwartz wasn't a big believer in prayer alone, so they brainstormed who else might take the milk if Verifine got surly. By the end of lunch, the short-list included Golden Guernsey down in Milwaukee; Borden, Dean Milk Company, and Bowman Dairy Company in the Chicago metro area; Foremost Farms out in Baraboo, near Madison; and Lake-to-Lake Dairy in Kiel.

Mary recited the jingle, "*For Goodness Sake, Buy Lake-to-Lake.*"

Overdrive cracked, "You know, I've always wanted one of those skimpy-skirted Lake-to-Lake girls painted on the side of one of our silos."

❋ ❋ ❋

The May 4th NFO chapter meeting was standing room only. After Van Driest introduced him to the crowd, Schwartz provided an overview of the meeting with Papini. Most farmers present were relieved, since in the last day or two, they'd already received their second checks covering two month's-worth of milk.

Overdrive kept his eyes on Schwartz, as Van Driest

led the group through the rest of the meeting's business. Schwartz was scanning the room and reading the crowd. Based on the look on his face, Schwartz didn't like what he saw. As Van Driest was about to adjourn the meeting, Schwartz hopped up and whispered something in his ear. Van Driest nodded, and ceded the floor for one last announcement.

Schwartz, trying to hide his concern, "Just to be on the safe side, I recommend you all hand-carry those checks to your banks tomorrow, if you haven't already. Nobody should relax until those checks clear."

After a moment of stunned silence, someone shouted from the back, "I thought you told us Papini already had the money to back our checks."

Schwartz exhaled heavily, and said, "I told you that's what Papini said. I didn't say the money was there, for sure. There's a difference. If we have a problem, it's important we know sooner rather than later."

Another farmer jumped to his feet, "What happens if we have a problem?"

Schwartz, now grim, "We'll roll up our sleeves and work around the clock. I've seen this before, and know exactly what to do. We won't rest until the milk every one of you produces, is being paid for."

A third farmer shouted out, "Our milk was being paid for before you and the NFO ever came along."

Schwartz held up his hands in a placating gesture, "I hear you, but my focus is on what comes next, and yours should be too. If the checks clear, we stay the course. If not, we've got work to do."

Another farmer stood up, "I heard the NFO sent you to Minnesota, and you just got back today. Are you sticking around until we know?"

Schwartz nodded, "If the checks bounce, I'll be here for as long as it takes."

* * *

The next day about noon, the NFO trucks arrived at Papini's with the day's milk as usual, but the plant was shuttered. One of the drivers walked to the house and knocked, but no answer. Everything was dark and empty, and there'd been no people or vehicles anywhere in sight. One of the drivers went to a nearby home, and called Van Driest for advice. Van Driest was just sitting down to lunch with Schwartz. Having no other choice, they told the drivers to dump the milk.

Van Driest's knee-jerk reaction was to phone-chain the news to all farmers immediately, but Schwartz knew from experience that broadcasting a problem without any indication of how it'd be fixed, was a bad idea. He wanted the message to include, at the very least, a pledge that the NFO would do everything in its power to resolve the situation ASAP. Schwartz's first move was to call NFO-central, talk to the president, Oren Lee Staley, and get his blessing on the pledge. Schwartz's next move was to educate Van Driest on the importance of involving the banks now. In past situations, the banks feeling the most pain became the NFO's strongest allies. Banks understood the local business community better than anyone, and Schwartz knew he needed their help. When the phone-chain message went out, it paired the bad news with NFO's pledge, directed each farmer to tell their banker to call Van Driest, and told farmers to await further instructions concerning the next day's milk.

Van Driest's home became the NFO's war room, as

calls streamed in from bankers, and dozens of farmers hoping for more and better news. Schwartz's third move was to form a small working group. From experience, he knew he needed a small motivated group that could move fast. By motivated, he meant the banker and farmer that stood to lose the most if things went south. This line of reasoning led him to Oostburg Bank and Overdrive and Mary. Van Driest placed the calls and extended the invitations. Everyone agreed to join, and that evening they gathered at Van Driest's house, after the Evans family finished milking the cows.

* * *

For the rest of the day, Schwartz and Van Driest kicked around ideas on what to do. That evening, the president of Oostburg Bank, Peter Nyenhuis, was first to arrive. Given the gravity of the situation, Peter took the liberty of bringing along his attorney, Ted Ritter. The four sat in the living room and filled each other in until Overdrive and Mary arrived.

After exchanging pleasantries, the full group settled around the dining room table. There, complements of Mrs. Van Driest, sat a fresh pot of coffee and plate of coconut chocolate-chip bars. The oldest Van Driest son had built a home next door, and now ran the family farm with his father's help. On her way next door to give them some privacy, Mrs. Van Driest stopped by the dining room to see if her husband needed anything else. She put on a weak smile and nodded a greeting to everyone else, but chiseled to her face were the telltale signs of worry.

Van Driest thanked everyone for coming. During introductions, it came out that Overdrive and Mary banked with Peter, and also relied on Ted for legal counsel. Schwartz circled his hand, and said, "Excellent. Highly-motivated close-knit teams can stand and fight. That's exactly what we need right now."

Peter caught Schwartz's eye, "I hope you don't mind me bringing Ted uninvited. But for a financial institution as small as ours, it's serious business when 28 loan holders suddenly lose their income. I felt Ted's presence was necessary."

Van Driest gasped, "28 of the 36 are yours?"

Peter nodded, "That's right. Given all the banks in Sheboygan County, I find it pretty remarkable that we're holding the bag on almost 80 percent of the farmers that got caught up in this. That's nearly every dairy farmer we serve. Any idea on how that might've happened?"

Van Driest leaned back with his hand to his chin, and thought a moment, "Well, come to think of it, we've recently experienced an incredible surge in membership. And most of them come from right around your area ... Town of Holland, Wilson, and Lima." Then, Van Driest turned to Schwartz, and said, "Otto, I'm not sure you know him, but that NFO roaming rep you guys sent us was phenomenal. Once he hit the recruiting trail, new members came pouring in."

Lower jaw dropped and eyebrows up, Schwartz said, "What roaming rep? That's a pilot program. It isn't even authorized for Wisconsin yet."

Knocked back and bug-eyed, Van Driest blurted, "What? But that's not possible! Al Stone's been working with our chapter for months. Before that he'd been helping to organize an NFO chapter in Fond du Lac County. The farmer from Fondy told me Al Stone walked on water."

202 | PATRICK J. HUGHES

Ted's eyes narrowed, "What's that farmer's name?"

Hand to forehead, Van Driest thought for a moment, "Let me think. Yeah, that's it ... Ernie Baker. Sounds like Ernie Banks, so it's easy to remember."

Ted looked at Schwartz, "If it's all right with you, I'm going to have my PI see what he can find out about Al Stone and Ernie Baker."

Schwartz nodded, "Please do."

Dread building inside, Overdrive wondered out loud, "Why'd we zero in on Papini? Locally, he's a complete unknown. There'd been plenty of other options. Around here, there's a cheese factory on every third or fourth country crossroads."

Van Driest, a trifle defensively, "Al ran across the opportunity while recruiting new members. Then, he and I met with Papini, and it seemed like a perfect fit. Papini's plant had ample refrigerated bulk-milk storage and cheese making facilities, and to get started, he'd been willing to pay a premium for milk. When NFO-central agreed to haul for free, it seemed like a no-brainer. The net to farmers diverting to Papini, was as good as they'd been getting from Verifine."

Mary shook her head, "I'm confused. Stone wasn't really associated with the NFO, yet he'd been able to arrange free NFO hauling?"

Van Driest shrugged, "Well, not exactly. Al reminded me the NFO was promoting free hauling, as a way to support market interventions. He encouraged me, as chapter president, to make the request. I did, and NFO-central approved."

Schwartz concurred, "When the NFO assigned me this case, they briefed me on the background. They'd thought it odd at the time, that a county chapter was charging off on its own, doing an intervention. But the NFO likes action, and goes out of its way to support it. Abe's right, they agreed to do the hauling. They also assigned a crackerjack negotiating team to deal with Verifine."

Ted had a thought, "Where can I find a copy of the agreement with Papini?"

Van Driest raised a hand, "I've got the original and a copy in my study. Let me fetch them, quick." The room fell silent until Van Driest returned, and handed Ted the copy.

Schwartz held up a finger, "Let me see the other one."

Van Driest fidgeted while they read, and volunteered, "Al told me the NFO's standard contract served as the basis of the agreement, and I shouldn't worry about it, because it's iron-clad."

Schwartz kicked back in his chair, looking back at Van Driest, "I've got news for you. This bears no resemblance to any NFO contract I've ever seen."

Ted frowned, and said, "I'd hope not. According to this language, recourse in case of breach falls only to the assets of Papini Cheese LLC. The corporate officers, presumably Vito Papini and perhaps others, are held harmless. If the LLC is a paper corporation with no assets, there's no recourse whatsoever."

Van Driest hung his head, "I don't know what to say, I really don't. Sorry doesn't even come close. It's just ... all the new members he brought in ... his finding a place to divert the milk ... the diversion's favorable milk price ... Al just drew me in, I guess. With this deal, I truly believed we'd have the staying power to force Verifine to pay more for our milk. After 50 years of dairy farming, I'd almost lost hope we'd ever see the day. Al sort of rekindled that hope."

Mary, in a soft voice, "Abe, this isn't all your fault. Every member voted to move forward. We were all taken in by Al Stone. Hell, we even gave that asshole a standing ovation at the end of the February meeting."

After a moment of empty air, Overdrive chimed in, "I agree with Mary. We were all duped, Abe. What I'd like to know is, where the hell did all that milk go? Two month's-worth of milk from three dozen farmers can't just disappear."

Schwartz rubbed his face with both hands, "That's a very good question."

Ted made another note, "I'll add to my PI's to-do list, looking into the whereabouts of the milk."

Heartened somewhat by the thought he wasn't solely to blame, Van Driest said, "We need to feed another message into the phone-chain. What'll it be?"

Peter said thoughtfully, "Realistically speaking, isn't the best possible outcome getting all these farmers back with Verifine at the same milk price as before? Perhaps the message needs to address how that'll happen. I mean, some of my farmers defaulted on their loans after one month without a milk check. They'll all probably default now."

Schwartz nodded, "I agree, we've lost our leverage, and it'd be a miracle to close a deal with Verifine before they found out. It's time to beg our way back to Verifine. But the NFO can't do the begging. Things have gotten testy between us. If we rolled over now, there'd be nothing stopping Verifine from pushing the price lower. It'd be better if each individual farmer had a conversation with them. Something along the lines of having second thoughts about the NFO approach, and asking to come back at the same price as before. You know, restore the longstanding positive relationship … that sort of thing. If it looks like farmers are giving up on the NFO, Verifine might snap at the chance to take them back."

Van Driest leaned forward, "Huh … so basically we tell everybody to dump tomorrow's milk, and have a hat-in-hand style conversation with Verifine pronto, so hopefully the following day they'd be back with them."

Peter chewed on his lower lip, then said, "I'd like to make a friendly amendment. Please instruct the farmers to get back to both you and their banks, on whether Verifine took them back."

Van Driest nodded, "I can do that."

The part about appearing to distance themselves from the NFO needed to be crystal-clear to the chapter members, and required explanation. Also, what was said to Verifine required the right tone and nuance, to have the greatest chance of success. The group helped Van Driest craft a message that got that done, then he picked up the phone and kicked off the chain.

CHAPTER 18

NFO Wipeout or Foul Play? – Friday; May 7, 1965; 9:00 PM

On Friday the farmers all dumped their milk again, and the second Papini checks started bouncing as expected. That evening, the working group convened once more. After everyone was settled, Van Driest cleared his throat, and said, "Otto and I have been glued to the phone all day. I'm afraid things have gone from bad to worse. Frankly, I'm feeling a little out of my depth, and believe it'd be best if Otto did most of the talking for us."

Schwartz exhaled heavily, and said, "We've heard from every farmer, and Verifine hasn't taken anyone back. James and Mary, I'd be interested in your firsthand account of how those conversations went."

Overdrive and Mary made eye contact, and Mary urged her husband to go first, "The guy we know best at Verifine is named Dan Steinke. He handles milk supplier services ... you know ... say you want to change the pickup time, you call Steinke. Anyway, his shift starts at 6:00 AM, so we called him a few minutes after. He sounded happy to hear from us, but said decisions like that were above his pay grade. He promised somebody would get back to us. About 9:00 AM we got a call back from a Jeff Klein, who said he worked directly for the president. We followed the script … had changed our mind, had lost faith in the NFO, and so on … but it didn't matter. Klein basically said Verifine wouldn't be taking us back."

Mary added, "We tried to get some sort of explanation, but Klein declined to give one, almost as though he'd been instructed not to. He was very apologetic, and you could tell he felt badly from the sound of his voice."

Peter leaned in and raised a finger, "Maybe I can provide some insight here. I'm acquainted with the president of Verifine, Marty De Schmitt, through the Sheboygan County Chamber of Commerce. He never struck me as the kind of guy who'd turn his back on hard-working farmers. It surprised me when by noon, I'd heard from a dozen farmers and all had been rejected. So, right after lunch I called De Schmitt directly." He looked around the room, then continued, "I hope I didn't step on anyone's toes by making that call."

Schwartz shook his head, "Fine by me."

Peter continued, "Well, De Schmitt said he fully understood the difficult position of those farmers, and genuinely felt terrible about it. After hearing this, him turning them away made no sense to me, so I kept pressing. He hemmed and hawed, but eventually spilled his guts. Afterward, he said he felt relieved to have told someone. When leaving home this morning, he opened the garage door, only to find a large box blocking his driveway. Inside, was the severed head of a Holstein, with a note that read ... *you'll be next, if you take back those NFO farmers*. De Schmitt is scared shitless. He doesn't know what to do."

Audible gasps ricocheted around the room, before it exploded in wild speculation ... *Is it the mob? Who else would do that?* ... and so on. Finally, Ted raised his voice, "Hey people, hold on! Before going off half-cocked, let's get all the facts on the table. The PI learned some interesting things today, too."

The room fell silent, and Ted continued, "This morning, the PI paid a visit to a Campbellsport-area farmer by the name of Ernie Baker. That's the guy who gave Abe the glowing endorsement of Al Stone. Baker was clearly caught off guard, but stuck to his story. The PI could tell things didn't add up ... there'd been no NFO sign in the yard, the farm was a mess, with dilapidated buildings, shit-caked cows, and so on. It just didn't look like the kind of farm that'd be owned, you know, by a farmer trying to organize a county-wide NFO chapter. So, the PI decided to stake the place out. He drove to the next road over, hiked back through a wooded lot, and positioned himself on a hill overlooking the farm with his binoculars. Soon after, he saw a man matching the description of Al Stone, drive a tractor into the yard. Stone appears to work for Baker. In fact, they share a certain likeness, and could even be brothers, or at least related."

Van Driest muttered, "You've got to be shitting me!"

Ted shook his head, "I'm not, and there's more. The PI spent the afternoon investigating the Papini plant, and talking to folks living nearby. Generally speaking, they'd been happy to see the plant reopen. But one man who'd worked there previously, was upset the old employees weren't hired back. He said he stopped by one day, and didn't recognize anybody. They weren't local. Also, several neighbors thought it odd that trucks were pulling in and out at all hours of the day and night. Daytime trucks had NFO logos, nighttime ones ... unmarked."

Schwartz held his head, "What the hell is going on here? Farmhands impersonating NFO reps ... cheese makers on the run ... bouncing checks ... disappearing milk ... severed heads. Can anybody help me connect the dots?"

Overdrive muttered, "I've got nothing."

Mary chimed in, "Me neither."

Peter said wisely, "It might be more productive for us to stay focused on finding a market for all that milk. Otherwise, more goes down the drain every day. It'll take a while to figure out what's going on, and we can deal with that later."

Ted nodded, "I agree with Peter. In the meantime, I'll take the action to investigate the LLC's corporate structure, and crack the whip on the PI. Let me see, his to-do list includes investigating Vito Papini ... finding out who has leverage over Bernie Baker and Al Stone ... discovering where the stolen milk went ... and identifying who gifted the severed head. Am I missing anything?"

Schwartz pursed his lips, "Verifine couldn't have hung on so long without finding an alternate source of milk. I'd like to know who that was. If not for them, we'd have inked a deal for a higher milk price by now."

Peter volunteered, "I'll call De Schmitt and ask. If we promise to help him out of his bind, I bet he'll tell me."

Schwartz bobbed his head, "You do that." Then he lowered his voice, "Okay, let's have some ideas on who might start buying all this milk." At the end of the discussion, Schwartz and Van Driest took the action to call all the dairies identified, and gauge their interest. The day's phone-chain message was simple ... *we're working on it and making progress, but dump tomorrow's milk.*

* * *

The next morning things began to pop, so Schwartz moved the working group meeting up to 2:00 PM. Once everyone had arrived and settled, Schwartz went around the room for updates. Peter was told by De Schmitt that they'd been able to hold out against the NFO, by buying Chicago-area spot market milk. Overdrive and Mary reported an unexpected visitor, in the form of an unmarked bulk-milk truck. The driver gave them an ABC Milk Haulers LLC contract to sign, and offered to load up their milk on the spot and haul it to Chicago. The contract was vague concerning who'd accept delivery and pay for the milk, saying only that potential-processors included, but weren't limited to, Borden, Dean, and Bowman. ABC promised best efforts to sell the milk at the prevailing spot market price, which again, wasn't specified. Under the terms, Overdrive and Mary were obligated to pay a specified hauling fee, whether or not the milk was sold.

Overdrive and Mary knew enough to call Ted, and read him the language over the phone, before doing anything. Ted told them to order ABC off their property, and then called Schwartz and Van Driest to pass along what'd happened. By then, dozens of calls had come in from confused farmers, wondering if ABC had been sent by the NFO, and whether they should sign. Immediately, a phone-chain message went out warning farmers not to sign with ABC. The message went on to say that great progress was being made on their behalf, and they'd all have legitimate processor contracts in a day or two, tops.

In an effort to back up that optimism, Schwartz ran a new idea past NFO-central. He proposed they team with Verifine to recruit one or more regional processors to pick up and store the NFO-member milk, which would then be double-shipped to Verifine. This way, De Schmitt could take back the NFO farmers, without getting himself killed. NFO-central approved of the idea, but advised they stick with Wisconsin-based dairies. Although the multiple reports were still unconfirmed, the NFO had received intel speculating the Chicago beverage milk markets were already mobbed-up. They feared the mob was now going after Wisconsin, with Papini and ABC at the point of the spear.

The theme of uniting to keep the mob out of Wisconsin resonated with the working group. Whether it'd appeal to Verifine and one or more of the other Wisconsin-based dairies was an open question. Peter called De Schmitt on the spot, and ran the idea past him. Mid-story, De Schmitt exploded at the mention of ABC, and identified them as Verifine's source of Chicago spot market milk.

Both ends of the line crackled, as they speculated on whether ABC had been Papini's night-hauler. As part of that, De Schmitt let slip he'd been paying ABC a premium over the pre-diversion raw milk price. Paying ABC more than his own local farmers threw Schwartz into a rage, and pretty soon De Schmitt and Schwartz were going after each other like a couple of pit bulls. Peter stepped in to try to restore the peace, Ted and Mary tried to help, Van Driest sat back in stunned silence, and Overdrive fled to the bathroom and threw cold water on his face, for fear of saying something he couldn't take back.

After tempers subsided and cooler heads prevailed, everyone agreed on the importance of working together to keep the mob at bay. De Schmitt was all-in on hard-selling the double-ship plan to the other Wisconsin dairies.

* * *

De Schmitt insisted on hosting a summit of Wisconsin-based dairies, and worked the weekend to set it up. The presidents of Lake-to-Lake, Golden Guernsey, and Foremost agreed to convene at Verifine for a meeting starting at 1:00 PM Monday May 9th. The farmers on the working group bowed out, but Schwartz, Peter and Ted spent the morning with De Schmitt, strategizing over how best to convince the visiting execs to join forces with them to repel a common enemy, the mob. The group insisted Ted do most of the talking, being a trained lawyer with a certain knack for persuasion.

After the introductions, Ted laid out the evidence, point by point. He had them at the severed head. Discussion turned to the rescue plan. De Schmitt produced a large map of Wisconsin, and on it, Foremost, Lake-to-Lake, and Golden Guernsey marked the locations, capacities, and current loadings of their refrigerated bulk-milk storage facilities and beverage-milk processing plants. Finding a home for all that milk, with Verifine staying behind-the-scenes, was a non-trivial problem. But after several hours of debate, a solution began to emerge.

Foremost was willing to help, but as it turned out,

Lake-to-Lake and Golden Guernsey were closer and had adequate slack capacities. These two dairies, Verifine, and the NFO agreed to a deal that essentially restored markets to their pre-diversion state, with a few superficial exceptions. Once the deal was struck, Schwartz called Van Driest, who used the phone-chain to call an emergency meeting of the NFO chapter for that night. The scripted message read ... *new processor contracts will be signed at the meeting ... milk pickups will commence tomorrow ... be sure to attend.*

Under the deal, trucks marked 'Lake-to-Lake' or 'Golden Guernsey' were to pick up the milk from the 36 farmers, and haul it to their own facilities. There, the milk would either be off-loaded to storage, or held temporarily in the parked trucks. Later, this same milk would be double-hauled to Verifine's plants, using the same trucks re-marked 'Verifine'. Marking and re-marking trucks wasn't an issue. Independent haulers served multiple dairies, and the use of magnetic decals had been standard practice for years. Contractually, the 36 farmers were divvied between Lake-to-Lake and Golden Guernsey. Then, through two dairy-to-dairy contracts, Verifine would buy back the milk of the 36.

Apt scheduling avoided operational impacts on Lake-to-Lake and Golden Guernsey, and the plan required only modest use of their facilities, so both granted Verifine this modest use for free. Hauling costs did rise as a result of the double-haul, and Verifine agreed to pay the increase. Farmers would receive a 10 cent per hundred-pound increase in the price paid for their milk, compared to pre-diversion. It wasn't much, but it was something. Although Lake-to-Lake and Golden Guernsey initially paid the higher milk price, they passed this cost

214 | PATRICK J. HUGHES

increase along to Verifine. Even with the higher hauling and milk costs, Verifine's total costs declined compared to what they'd been paying ABC during the diversion.

With their leverage long gone, the NFO felt fortunate to wrangle a 10 cent raise for their farmers. Even so, the hit taken by each farmer was staggering. Over two month's-worth of their milk had been stolen, and they'd been dumping milk daily since the scam came to light. Although their milk had a market starting tomorrow, the first checks from Lake-to-Lake or Golden Guernsey wouldn't arrive until early June.

Nobody felt good about the farmer's plight. But with time running out, nothing more could be done before tonight's emergency meeting, so they pressed on with getting ready for it. The Lake-to-Lake and Golden Guernsey execs called back to their offices, and arranged for the hand-delivery of their standard processor contracts. Before the meeting, these contracts needed to be copied, and duplicates filled in by hand for each farmer. Then, at the meeting, each party would sign both, and walk away with their own hardcopy. Horsepower was needed to complete this blizzard of paperwork, so Verifine bribed a few admins with overtime to stay late. Meanwhile, Verifine's attorney drafted the two dairy-to-dairy contracts, and revised them to the satisfaction of Lake-to-Lake and Golden Guernsey. These contracts were executed on the spot.

Once the admin production line was underway, the dairy execs and Schwartz, Peter and Ted debated how best to handle the meeting. They decided on a story that meshed with what the farmers already knew, and provided a positive path forward. Messaging needed to avoid creating momentum for costly actions with uncertain outcomes, such as a lawsuit against Papini Cheese LLC. A delicate balance was needed to defend the NFO's reputation, while admitting the diversion had failed and resulted in significant losses to participating farmers. Lake-to-Lake and Golden Guernsey would naturally come across as white knights, but in reality Verifine was paying the freight behind the scenes, and needed to be treated fairly. There'd be no mention of the mob whatsoever. Farmers had enough worries without adding the specter of the mob to their list.

✳ ✳ ✳

Every farmer was present and the room abuzz, when Van Driest, Schwartz, Peter, Ted and the presidents of Lake-to-Lake and Golden Guernsey walked into the room. Van Driest made introductions, and gave Schwartz the floor. The way Schwartz spun it, negotiations with Verifine had understandably broken down once word got out that Papini was insolvent. Verifine would've loved to have taken them back, but by then they'd already found alternate milk supplies, and contractually, their hands had been tied. Needing another solution, the NFO proceeded to arrange for Lake-to-Lake and Golden Guernsey to take the milk. Schwartz emphasized that these dairies weren't signing contracts with the NFO, but rather with each individual farmer. This particular market intervention had failed, but as Schwartz put it, the NFO would continue to pursue collective bargaining opportunities for the betterment of family dairy farms.

When a rumble of discontent began to build, Schwartz quickly dampened it by saying the dairies came with contracts to be signed, they're offering Verifine's old price plus 10 cents, and milk pickups would begin tomorrow. The few farmers that'd signed with ABC were advised to order ABC off their property tomorrow, and refer any complaints to Attorney Ted Ritter, who'd handle the problem at the NFO's expense. That evening 36 farmers went home with a new processor contract, but also a deep anger and resentment toward the NFO, over the losses they'd suffered. Nobody had been physically injured at the meeting, but there'd been plenty of hostility in the room.

CHAPTER 19

Farmers Fall and Bank Teeters – Monday;
May 10, 1965; 4:30 PM

Just prior to closing-time on Monday, Peter received a courier-delivered letter from the banking division of the Wisconsin Department of Financial Institutions. According to an anonymous complaint, Oostburg Bank had impaired capital due to a flurry of recent loan defaults. The state's bank examiners would arrive at 9:00 AM the next morning to investigate. Peter called Ted, who in turn called Van Driest looking for Schwartz, only to learn that Schwartz had already left the state. Ted tracked Schwartz down, but he couldn't return for three days.

As promised, the state's examiners invaded Oostburg Bank the next morning. They found 28 dairy farm loans to be in default. Following the state's standard procedures for fairly valuing loans, the asset values of these loans were slashed. From then on, it was simply a matter of doing the math. By the end of the day, the examiners officially notified the bank of its insolvency due to impaired capital. The bank had 30 days to resolve the issue, or face liquidation.

Peter was beside himself and didn't know what to do. That evening, he and Ted had dinner. Ted promised to study the statutes that night, and get back to him first thing in the morning. When Peter picked up the early-bird call, Ted said grimly, "There's an appeals process, but you need a basis for one. You've a 10-day window to file it with the banking institutions review board, which is also part of the Department of Financial Institutions. The appeal needs to state the grounds of the objection to the banking division's order. The review board will hold a hearing, but there's nothing firm in the law about how quickly. The board has the power to stay the order in the meantime, but we don't know that they would. Do you have the basis for an appeal?"

Peter exhaled heavily, and said, "None that I can think of. If those 28 loans stay in default, they're right. We're short on capital."

Ted, probing in a new direction, "Well, maybe not. You can issue an assessment on all outstanding shares of stock, and raise enough money to resolve the capital shortfall. Have you ever done that before?"

Peter muttered, "No, I haven't. But I'm familiar with the process. It takes some time. You work backward from when you absolutely must have the money, cut that in half, and call it a deadline. Rumor has it, responses are always late. In our case, a lot of our shareholders won't be able to come up with the money."

Ted, now focused, "Okay, say a shareholder can't ante up. Then, you've got the right to auction their shares in a public sale. You'd pick the highest bidders, and the buyers would ante up the assessment plus whatever they bid for the shares. The share-sale proceeds cover the cost of the sale, and the original shareholders get what's leftover. If that's less than they originally paid, too bad for them."

Despondent, Peter said, "True, but that takes time too. Among other things, you need to post copies of the notice of sale in 5 public places, at least 10 days in advance of when sealed bids are due."

Ted thought about that, "Huh. Well, if we required sealed bids to be in the form of cashier's checks, at least we'd get the money right away."

The discussion went on like this for another hour. Ted sketched timelines for the various options based on the statutory requirements. To these, he and Peter penciled in details for what'd have to be done by when. As it turned out, Peter's best bet was to initiate the assessment on shareholders immediately. Then he'd know sooner rather than later if a stock sale was required, leaving time to complete one. During the brainstorming, they came up with a better solution involving the NFO, and planned to give Schwartz the hard sell as soon as he returned.

❋ ❋ ❋

Ted, Peter, and Schwartz met at Ted's law office in Random Lake, on the morning of May 13th. After filling Schwartz in on what'd happened since he left, Ted and Peter moved on to their hard-sell strategy, which began by ripping Schwartz a new asshole.

Ted and Peter laid it on thick ... *the NFO can't simply walk away from a failed milk diversion ... it's ruined three dozen dairy farmers ... it'll soon bring down a bank ... none of this would've happened if not for the NFO ... it doesn't matter that an imposter set it up, that simply highlights the NFO's flagrant lack of chapter oversight ... as far as 36 wronged farmers are concerned, the whole thing was NFO-led* ... and so on. Peter swore he'd whip up the entire Midwest's banking community and drive the NFO out of existence, if they didn't make it right.

Schwartz was a big boy and stood his ground, but they'd succeeded in getting his attention. Soon, the discussion turned to what actions the NFO might consider. Ted and Peter lobbied hard for the NFO to work with its members, and somehow bring all the farm loans out of default before the state liquidated Oostburg Bank. If the farmers caught up on their loans, the bank would again be solvent and all of this would go away. Schwartz promised the problem would have his undivided attention, and said he'd do his best to get NFO-central to act in time.

* * *

That evening Overdrive and Mary called Ted for advice. Their Oostburg Bank loan was in default, and the early June Lake-to-Lake check wouldn't be large enough to catch them up. Before starting to borrow from Peter to pay Paul, they wanted to know if he had a better idea. Ted filled them in on the bank's troubles, and what Schwartz was trying to do. He advised them to wait and see if Schwartz was successful.

In recent days, Ted had been plagued by a persistent recurring thought. The call from Overdrive and Mary brought this thought front and center. Curious, he asked, "Has it occurred to you that more than the mob might be behind all this?"

Overdrive blurted, "You mean Rachel Wolf?"

Ted sighed, "Exactly. I thought maybe I was just being paranoid."

Mary said solemnly, "We've been talking about it. How else could so many of the farmers caught up in this mess, bank at Oostburg? What's Peter think?"

"You know, I've never asked him. Hang on a minute, I'll call him on the other line." He set down the handset, and for the next few minutes, sounds could be heard in the background. When he returned, Ted said, "We've all had the same thought, so maybe there's something to it. But for now, let's keep this little conspiracy theory to ourselves. It might confuse things with the NFO, and in any event, it doesn't change what Peter and I have to do."

* * *

The bank's clock had started ticking on May 11th ... 10-days to the appeals deadline ... 30-days to problem resolution or liquidation. Shareholders received hand-carried assessment demands from the bank on May 14th. Peter and Ted only gave them five days to respond, to keep open the possibility of a resolution through the appeals process. If the assessment raised sufficient capital, the fact that the bank was once again solvent could serve as the grounds for appeal.

Over those five days the bank's board, Peter, and Peter's staff spent untold hours on the phone pleading with shareholders. Even so, when the deadline passed, assessments had been received for only one-third of the outstanding shares. A few more trickled in over the next few days, but when the appeals window expired on May 21st, only 40 percent of the required capital had been raised.

To better understand this disappointing outcome, Peter and Ted took Peter's closest friend among shareholders to Sunday brunch the next day. After learning the reason for the free meal, the friend handed Peter a letter he'd received by hand-delivery, the day after the bank's assessment demand arrived. The anonymous letter promised a tidy profit to any shareholder that turned in their shares for public sale, rather than pay the assessment. The letter was signed *Wealthy and Watching*, and had no return address.

After brunch, Peter and Ted called around to other shareholders, and they'd all received that letter. Ted muttered, "It smells like Rachel Wolf."

Peter snapped, "It sure as hell does. Now what? If we go ahead with the sale, she'll own the bank."

Ted exhaled heavily, "If we don't go ahead, the bank gets liquidated."

❋ ❋ ❋

The next day, first thing in the morning, Peter and Ted checked in with Schwartz at NFO-central. Ted filled him in on the failure of the assessment. Then, in a low-pitched growl, Peter said, "God damn it Otto, we're either going to be liquidated or taken over by a hostile party. Is the NFO going to get off its ass, or not? We're running out of time here."

Schwartz admitted, "I've come up with a proposal that'd have NFO-central bring all the farmer's loans out of default. But it's been on Oren Lee's desk for days now, and that's not like him. I fear he'll balk."

Peter snapped, "Balk! Are you kidding me? I swear,

community bankers will ruin him and the NFO if he balks."

Schwartz grimaced, "I know, I know. I've told him that, but it just comes across like me talking. I'm running out of ideas."

Peter thought about that, then said, "Well, would it help if I had the president of the Independent Community Bankers of America call him? We're fishing buddies. Go steelhead fishing together every year up near Cheboygan, Michigan. I'm sure he'd be happy to do it. And he and the ICBA can be real assholes when they need to be. You know … light a fire under old Oren Lee … explain how they'll exterminate his pathetic organization if he doesn't step up."

Schwartz agreed, if a bit grudgingly, "Awww … geeezzz. I guess so. But make sure he doesn't mention my name."

Peter, voice still cold, "Give me the direct-line number. Then go hide in a bunker until you hear the boom. I guarantee it'll be a big one." Peter's friend picked up on the second ring, and said he'd make the call as soon as they hung up.

✽ ✽ ✽

Having no choice, Peter and Ted went ahead with the stock sale. They couldn't rely on the NFO coming through, and though chances were slim, they hoped somebody might out-bid Wolf. They placed the required public notices everywhere in Oostburg, and in a 'Hail Mary' attempt to attract bigger fish than Wolf, they also ran week-long announcements in the Chicago Tribune, Milwaukee Journal, Wisconsin State Journal,

224 | PATRICK J. HUGHES

and Sheboygan Press.

The 30-day liquidation clock would expire June 10th, so Ted scheduled the sealed bid opening for June 8th. Offerors were required to specify the number of shares they desired to purchase, and enclose a cashier's check covering the full amount for the shares plus assessment. In case the NFO came through, Ted made it clear the bank retained the right to decline all offers. If the bid opening put Wolf in control of the bank, the bank's board would have to choose their poison ... decline all bids and be liquidated, or roll over to Wolf. Peter scheduled the state's bank examiners for a return visit on June 9th at 9:00 AM. If the NFO failed and nobody outbid Wolf, they could always cancel if the board preferred liquidation over Wolf.

CHAPTER 20

Rachel's End Game – Tuesday; May 11, 1965; 5:00 PM

W hen the Oostburg Bank stock sale hit the street, Rachel was ready to go in for the kill. She'd studied every Upper Midwest community bank stock sale over the past five years. She'd identified a group of peer banks, meaning they had profiles similar to Oostburg's. For each peer bank, she'd found the highest market-clearing stock price received, and the date of transaction. Then, she'd escalated these values from their transaction dates to the present, to make them comparable. The present values across all peer banks provided the share-price range that Oostburg Bank could reasonably expect to receive, as a result of their stock sale.

Rachel was determined that Oostburg Bank wouldn't slip away again. To maximize her chances, she decided to adopt a two-tier, base and contingent, bidding strategy. Under this approach, she offered to acquire all the available shares at the base bid price. But at the same time, she also offered to acquire all the available shares at a higher contingent bid price, in the event that a rival bid exceeded her base offer. In other words, her base bid held sway unless another offer exceeded it, in which case her contingent bid held sway. Rachel chose the highest price received by any peer bank as her baseline, and then set her base and contingent bids at 25 and 50 percent over baseline, respectively.

There was good news and bad news for Rachel, when the terms and conditions of the stock sale came out in the public notice. On the plus side, there'd been nothing in it to prevent her from submitting a two-tiered bid. On the down side, bids in the form of cashier's checks were required. If she stuck with the two-tiered approach, Rachel would have to include cashier's checks for both options. The fact that one or the other, not both, would be selected didn't matter. She'd have to raise enough cash to cover both the base and contingent offers. This was a heavy lift, even for Rachel.

Although the financial challenge gave her pause, Rachel decided to persevere with the two-tier approach. She wanted to own those bastards at Oostburg Bank no matter what. It was a scramble, but by the time the checks were needed she managed to convert enough of her wealth to cash to cover them.

* * *

From the public sale notice, Rachel knew about 60 percent of Oostburg Bank's stock was in play, and sealed bids would be opened June 8th. But just to be safe, she also kept in regular touch with her insider at the banking division. From him, she learned that on June 9th, the day before the liquidation deadline, the state's bank examiners would again be onsite at Oostburg Bank. The news brought a most wicked and feral grin to her face. When the examiners declared the bank once again solvent on June 9th, she'd control it with 60 percent of the shares.

In Rachel's world, September 29th 1964 would forever be remembered as a day of infamy. On that day, James and Mary Evans scuttled her casino plans with the help of a half-breed spy, country lawyer, and small-town bank. To add to the day's humiliation, the half-breed's insurance company had even forced her to pay his fire losses.

Rachel swore that one day she'd make them all pay for what they'd done. She now knew June 9th 1965 was the day she'd begin to extract her revenge. On that day, she'd become controlling owner of Oostburg Bank, and begin a relentless campaign to hound the Evans family off their farm. Also on that day, Darkwater Flint would get his due. After that, she looked forward to rolling over Ritter Law, in the same manner generations-of-Wolfs had done before her. She knew the Evans family would try to fight back with Ritter. But Ritter wouldn't be up to the task, the Ritters never were. No, she'd drive the Evans's off their farm, and then she'd build her casino. It was inevitable, they just didn't know it yet.

Rachel picked up the phone, and dialed Vince. With a gleeful lilt in her voice, she said, "Vince, I've finally got a date … it's June 9th … on that day, have Phil's doer put Flint down like the dog he is."

CHAPTER 21

Team Overdrive Rallies but Takes a Hit –
Wednesday; June 2, 1965; 4:00 PM

Peter and Ted were beginning to panic. Sealed bids were rolling in, bid opening was fast approaching, yet no word from Schwartz and the NFO. They got Schwartz on the phone, and Peter demanded, "Any news, we're dying here!"

Schwartz, hyped and breathing hard, "He signed off! Oren Lee signed off! That call from your pal at the ICBA really did the trick. Oren Lee made some changes, but I think it'll still work."

Ted, impatient, "Otto, stop babbling and tell us what you've got."

Schwartz took a breath, "Okay, okay … how to say it … let me see." He calmed himself, then said, "The NFO will bring every farmer's loan current by paying the banks directly. I fought for these payments to be grants, but I lost. We'll only waive repayment on half the money. The other half we'll loan the farmers interest free, with repayments waived for the first 24 months. Thereafter, the farmers will need to repay the NFO in equal installments over a 12-month period."

Ted interjected, "The theory, then, is once the farmers are caught up on their bank loans, they'll be able to stay that way?"

Schwartz said wisely, "I don't see why not. They're being paid a higher price for their milk than before, and they don't pay the NFO a dime for two years."

Peter thought about that, then said, "How fast can this happen?"

Schwartz exhaled heavily, "That's potentially a problem. The money is in hand, but now with the loan and repayment component, farmers will need to sign a loan agreement before the NFO pays off their bank loan deficit."

Ted thought out loud, "With the phone-chain, Van Driest can set up an emergency chapter meeting in a hurry. How quickly can you get here with contracts and cashier's checks for all 36 farmers?"

The discussion went on like this for another half hour. They'd have Van Driest invite both the farmers and their bankers to the emergency meeting. That way, Peter could leave the meeting with his 28 cashier's checks. Say the meeting was held the night of June 6th, that'd leave enough time on June 7th to process the checks and update the loan ledgers. Then, Peter would know where he stood on June 8th, when the bids were opened. If all went well, on June 9th the bank examiners would find every loan current, and declare the bank once again solvent. If that happened, Peter could decline all the bids because the crisis was over. Peter and Ted stood firm on June 6th as the date for the emergency meeting, and after some grousing, Schwartz agreed to be there with contracts and cashier's checks.

The chapter meeting was a sight to behold. From the farmer's perspective, they walked in defaulted on their bank loans, and still livid from the loss of over two month's-worth of milk. The farmers blamed the NFO, and its lack of oversight, for allowing the heist to occur. None of them had a clue how to get out of the red. Walking out, every farmer was caught up at the bank, only half the money fronted to get them there needed to be repaid, and for the other half, the NFO gave them a sweetheart loan.

When Schwartz finished delivering the news, cheers erupted, hats flew into the air, and grown men and women laughed and cried for joy at the same time. Over the course of the meeting, the NFO went from pariah to GOAT, as in greatest of all time. Three dozen farmers went home with a rekindled flicker of hope for a brighter future. Just as important, a handful of bankers went home with cashier's checks. Among them Peter, who carried 28.

* * *

The next few days unfolded as Peter and Ted had hoped. The checks were cashed, and farm loan ledgers updated. The NFO's infused funds were now in the books and secure. On June 8th, Peter and Ted unsealed the bids to discover their worst nightmare had been true. Rachel Wolf's base bid was the highest received, placing her in control of the bank if bids were accepted. Had the NFO not come through, the bank's choices would've been to liquidation or cede control to Wolf.

On June 9th the state's bank examiners returned to Oostburg Bank. Following their standard procedures, they restored the asset values of the 28 dairy farm loans.

By the end of the day, Peter received official notification that his bank was solvent once more.

Ted and Peter were about to break out the champaign, when Overdrive and Mary called. With a tremble in his voice, Overdrive said, "Darkwater's been shot! They're not sure he'll make it."

Peter gasped, "What? Why?"

Ted slapped a palm to his forehead, "Of course! God damn it, why didn't I see that coming? That bitch penciled today as payback time for last September."

Mary gasped, "You think that's what all this's been about, all along? This entire NFO diversion mess? Getting back at us for last September?"

Ted snapped, "What else could it be?"

Peter, astonished, "But what about the mob?"

Ted shrugged, "At this point, I don't know."

Overdrive cursed, "Shit! Last September, we never should've let her go."

Ted muttered, "Well, we didn't let her go, per se. We all wanted to get on with our lives. We fired off a few warning shots, you know, the one-two punch, to encourage her to leave us alone. We presumed she was sane."

Peter, in a voice of regret, "Well, apparently we were wrong."

CHAPTER 22

Team Overdrive Moves on to Plan B –
Wednesday; June 9, 1965; 11:00 AM

D arkwater was at his current base camp, on an island in one of the more remote bodies of water among the chain of lakes in the Eagle River area. He'd been busy all morning making preparations for the afternoon's fishing expedition. Clients, regulars of his, were up from Chicago through the coming weekend. Fishing in recent days had been exceptional, and weather conditions continued to be right. Lunker smallmouth bass were in the midst of a feeding frenzy on crayfish. He made sure to pack spare underwear and trousers. One of yesterday's clients had literally shit-his-pants after hooking a monster. As usual, he left the live bait until last, so it'd be as fresh as possible when he and the flatlanders hit the lake.

Darkwater believed in using native crayfish for bait. He'd seen firsthand the problems invasive species could cause, and didn't trust what bait dealers were selling. To have a ready supply of native crayfish, he set up his own natural farm. Years ago, he'd fenced a large area lousy with crayfish, using fine-mesh galvanized steel netting. The fenced area had a rocky/gravelly bottom at a five-to-ten-foot depth, and was adjacent to a cattail marsh in the back of a cove.

To avoid having to surface repeatedly for air while catching crayfish, Darkwater had permanently installed a makeshift breathing tube. It consisted of a long hollow cane pole, with the bottom end fitted to a length of surgical tube. The tube had a squeeze valve at the very end. The top end of the cane pole was hidden among the cattails, and fastened to them with rope to keep the opening well above water level. When gathering crayfish, Darkwater would pop the valve into his mouth, and use his jaw muscles to squeeze it between his teeth when he needed air.

For short trips like popping over to the cove for bait, Darkwater used a small ancient row boat. He enjoyed the quiet and serenity of rowing, but time was tight today, so he fired up the stern-mounted outboard and reversed away from shore. The morning was sunny but with a chill, so he wore baggy jeans and a hoodie over his swim trunks. After the dive, he'd need to strip off the trunks, dry, and redress so he brought a large beach towel. As he shifted to forward and turned the boat, he took in the panoramic view and smiled to himself. There was nowhere else on earth he'd rather be.

* * *

As he entered the cove, Darkwater cutoff the outboard and glided silently forward, so as not to disturb his crayfish prey. He frequented this place and had a feel for it, some might say a mystical feel. On this morning, something just felt off in the cove. By instinct, his senses elevated to high-alert. Momentum slowly carried the boat over the fenced area. Just as he dropped anchor, he glimpsed something odd. After a double-take, he recognized the sun's reflection off the flat stern of a poorly hidden john boat on the far shore ... a boat that shouldn't have been there. As he turned to get a better look, the flash of a gun barrel's unmistakable reflection caught his eye ... pointed straight at him. Instinctively, Darkwater ducked low and rolled over the gunnel away from the gun. The shot rang out an instant before he splashed into the water.

Treading water with his head hidden behind the boat, Darkwater felt a strange burning sensation in his right bicep. When he looked, he saw the through-and through holes in the sleeve, and the beginnings of blood in the water ... shit! Then, he heard the john boat launch ... shit, shit ... they're coming! Seeing no reachable safe havens after a desperate head spin, Darkwater took a deep breath and dove. His mind raced ... what to do? Frantically, he scanned the fenced area ... shit, shit, shit ... no place to hide! But he got an idea when he saw the breathing tube ... play dead! Using his legs and one good arm, Darkwater awkwardly settled to the bottom face-down, popped the valve into his mouth, and breathed.

Darkwater's body was buoyant, and he desperately searched for something, anything, to keep it down. The john boat would be on him any minute, and he'd better be motionless by then. No root to grab, no boulder ... shit ... nothing but small rocks. Wait ... small rocks! In a furious rush, he stuffed his hoodie-pouch and jeans-pockets with them, and that did the trick. His mind raced as he took one last look around ... shit ... the water's crystal-clear, could they see the tube? He eased his body sideways to cover the tube. Cane pole? It'll blend in with the cattails, it'll have to. Oh-oh, here he comes. Relax ... breathe ... don't move.

The john boat's shadow stopped next to the one from his boat. Darkwater willed his body to breath easily without movement ... shit, shit, shit ... the bubbles! He drew in air from the breathing tube, but exhaled to the water. His mind raced ... could he exhale back through the tube? Not for long, he guessed. He'd be re-breathing the same air, and eventually it'd be oxygen depleted. He decided to edge forward slightly, until tight to the cattails. Bubbles coming up through them would be less obvious. What the hell is that guy doing next to my boat?

Darkwater concentrated on the movements above. Interesting, somebody just jumped into my boat. There must be two of them, because the john boat's unanchored and its outboard is still idling. Hmmm ... sounds like my anchor going up. Huh ... that's my outboard. Oh-oh, he's puttering my boat out of the cove. Wait a minute, I know that roar, that's my outboard wide-open. What the hell, he's coming back ... fast! Just then, Darkwater's boat crashed into the cattails at top speed, and eventually came to a stop and went silent. Huh ... hiding my boat, I guess. What's all the splashing? Hmmm ... must be the guy swimming back to the john boat. Yeah, that's it. There's his shadow being pulled in.

Slowly, the john boat's shadow drifted in Darkwater's direction. What? Really? You're going to shoot me some more? Helpless, Darkwater laid motionless on the bottom. He concentrated on letting every muscle go slack, and chanted ... *dead men don't jerk ... if shot don't jerk ... relax ... breath ... don't move.*

Suddenly multiple piercing-burning sensations ripped through his torso, followed by the muffled underwater garble of gunfire ... two shots. He willed himself to remain motionless ... aaauuuggghhh ... hang on ... aaauuuggghhh ... hang on. The shadow hovered over him for what seemed like an eternity, looking for signs of life. But other than swirling blood, nothing moved, and eventually the outboard throttled-up and the boat roared away.

* * *

Once sure the john boat was gone, Darkwater unloaded the rocks from his pockets, and crawled up the cane pole into the cattail marsh. His only chance for survival was getting to the boat. Mind-numbing pain had long since replaced burning sensations. It helped to bite on his hood, as he waded tentatively through the marsh. Once at the boat, he flopped in over the side, and examined his wounds. All three were through-and-through, and seeping blood. The arm seemed to be a flesh wound, but both torso shots had cracked ribs and probably done worse. With his teeth and good arm, he shredded the beach towel into strips, and used them to stem the bleeding as best he could. Then, he fired up the outboard, and after multiple back-and-forth reversals was able to churn his way out of the marsh, and head toward base camp.

While out on the water, Darkwater once again bit down hard on his soaked hood, to help manage the pain. He thanked the spirits for watching over him, and for blessing water with the ability to diffract light. If not for that, he knew he'd be a dead man. How else could a skilled shooter miss two kill-shots at point-blank range? As base camp came into sight, Darkwater began to fade. While still able, he pointed the boat at the landing area, and used a towel strip to lash the tiller in place to hold that course. Before passing out, he saw a resort-owned boat approaching with his afternoon clients, and gave thanks that the spirits had more help to give.

Darkwater ran his guide business out of an Eagle River resort owned by Barney Swanson. Swanson liked to get out into the wild when he could, and given that Wednesdays were slow, decided today he'd ferry Darkwater's clients to base camp himself. When the island base-camp came into view, Swanson knew instantly something was wrong ... Darkwater's row boat was missing. Anxious, he pushed the throttle up a notch and scanned the area. Soon, the row boat came into view, also headed toward base-camp's landing. It came from the direction of the crayfish farm, which made sense, so Swanson relaxed and eased up on the throttle. It'd be best if his friend landed first. That way, he'd be there to greet his clients like he always did. That line of thinking changed, when Darkwater slumped over.

Swanson watched in horror as the row boat ran aground without slowing, and stuck there with the outboard still churning. He shouted for the flatlanders to hang on, as he spun a quick circle, aimed for shore, and goosed the engine. The maneuver caused the front of the boat to plane upward. After the leading tip slid onto dry land, he jerked the outboard back to neutral and killed it, then ran the length of the boat and jumped off before it came to a stop. A second later, he killed Darkwater's outboard and shouted for help to carry his friend.

As the clients scrambled out of one boat and onto

the other, Swanson inspected the blood-stained bandages and muttered ... *shit, they found him!* The three men gingerly carried Darkwater to shore, and then onto the other boat. Once all were settled, Swanson pushed off, jumped on, and made it to the back of the boat in several leaps. The outboard sprang to life, and was at full throttle before completing its turn from shore. The flatlanders peppered him with questions about what happened to Trophy Hound, but Swanson shrugged and stayed silent.

During the journey, Swanson's mind raced as he tried to remember what he'd been told to do, if this day ever came. Darkwater had coached him, but that'd been over eight months ago. Slowly, it came back to him. The police ... local, county or tribal ... were not to be trusted. He should assume his resort was under surveillance, and couldn't go there. He needed to keep Darkwater away from local hospitals and medical clinics. He was to call Robin Thunder, nothing more. She'd know what to do, and would take it from there. He glanced at his friend and thought some more, then came to a decision. He changed the heading of the boat slightly. Destination? ... the private dock nearest the remote cabin where Darkwater and Robin lived. Then, he prayed that she'd be home. For the rest of the journey, Swanson wondered what to do with the flatlanders, after his friend was in Robin's care. Huh ... it's a nice day, might as well take them fishing.

* * *

Robin was home, and knew exactly what to do. She called Make Wit, the elder of the Little Prairie Band of the Potawatomi. The tribe couldn't be trusted, but the same wasn't true of their band. Robin was panicked, so Make

Wit calmed her down, drew from her the information he needed, and told her to sit tight by the phone. Then one after the other, he dialed an excellent country doctor and two band-member confidants, Round Wind and Cedar Root. The doctor agreed to treat Darkwater, and the band members were dispatched to transport him. Afterward, Make Wit called Robin, and comforted her until his men arrived.

Gunshot wounds, especially accidental ones during hunting season, were common in the north. In most of these cases, neither the careless fools nor the victims wanted word to get out. This particular doctor served such a clientele, and understood the importance of discretion. He performed surgery right in his home, and even provided after-care services there, for as long as needed. The surgery went well, and the multiple internal injuries were all repairable. Darkwater had lost a lot of blood, but Robin, Round Wind, and Cedar Root all donated and he pulled through. Darkwater was lucky to be alive, and had a long recovery ahead of him.

❉ ❉ ❉

After almost a month, Darkwater was finally up to seeing visitors. Ted borrowed his church's van, and Overdrive, Mary, Old Bill, and Peter joined him for the ride north. Still taking every precaution, the Little Prairie Band directed them to a secluded location, covered their heads in sacks, and transferred them to other vehicles. When the sacks were removed, they were standing in the main room of what appeared to be a large rustic cabin, at the foot of Darkwater's bed.

Darkwater was pale and weak. Pleasantries were

kept to a minimum to preserve his energy, and Ted got right to the point, "Last September we had a meeting much like this one, to decide what to do about Rachel Wolf. Darkwater wanted his old life back, and needed the insurance payout to get back on his feet. James and Mary wanted to get back to running their farm. Peter's bank wasn't in a position to bankroll a lengthy litigation process. Old Bill questioned whether Wolf could be taken down by a country lawyer, a small independent bank, one dairy farm family, and a sportsmen's guide. A lot has happened since then. I'd like to go around the room, and see where everybody stands today. Who wants to go first?"

Darkwater wiggled a finger, and said in a weak voice, "I've been living like a fugitive since September, and they still found me. I can't live like this anymore."

Overdrive cleared his throat, "Mary and I've discussed this. We're pretty certain that once Wolf had control of Oostburg Bank, she'd have found a way to beat us out of our farm. We're still the only thing standing between her and a casino gold mine. This'll never end unless we can put her behind bars."

Peter raised his hand, "The bank's board unanimously supports seeking to put Wolf behind bars. Financially it's still a problem for us, but things are different now. Verifine and the NFO were burned in this last go round, and Lake-to-Lake, Golden Guernsey, and Foremost also got a taste of what the future holds if nothing is done. We can do this, if they step up and help."

Ted turned to the most senior among them, "Old Bill, what do you think?"

Old Bill grinned back, "My opinion hasn't changed. I still think it'll take more than us in this room to bring down Rachel Wolf."

THE END

ACKNOWLEDGEMENT

The authentic setting and family dynamics of the Overdrive Evans series stems from the author's upbringing on a family dairy farm near Cascade, in Sheboygan County, Wisconsin. In addition to my family, everyone living in the area during the mid-1960s contributed to the milieu, and I'd like to acknowledge them all.

Special thanks go to those who made specific contributions. I relied on the early childhood development expertise of Dr. Paula Hughes to associate the toddler character, Jake, with age-appropriate language and motor skills. Tim Vane once again provided an excellent review of the draft manuscript. Without the assistance of Michael Hughes, the life-threatening scene involving the character Old Bill could not have been written. The plot relies on how state banks in Wisconsin are regulated, and Jerry Weinhold pointed me toward sources on that topic.

My previous novel, Headwaters Deception, was my debut and also the first in the Overdrive Evans series. Readers too numerous to mention sent me emails on what they did and didn't like about my debut. These suggestions were incredibly helpful, and contributed mightily to this effort. Readers, please keep those emails coming to patrick.j.hughes@outlook.com!

ABOUT THE AUTHOR

Patrick J. Hughes

Patrick J. Hughes is a husband, father, writer, and retired research engineer. He was raised on a dairy farm and went on to become the first member of his family to graduate from college, earning two degrees from the University of Wisconsin-Madison and another from Stanford. He spent his long career fighting climate change while employed at a major research university, large and small consulting firms, and a leading national laboratory. He traveled the world during his career, but never forgot where he came from. He currently resides in Oak Ridge, TN, with his wife, Paula, and together they have two grown sons, Jared and Zach.